List of books by Roger Carpenter

Rutland's Curse
1879 treachery in Afghanistan

Rutland's Guns 1900
Action and tragedy in South Africa

Rutland's Blues and Greys
1863 the American Civil War

All these books are available from Amazon.co.uk and Amazon.com.

www.roger-carpenter.co.uk

Rutland's Blues and Greys

A year of the American Civil War

Roger Carpenter

authorHOUSE®

AuthorHouse™ UK Ltd.
500 Avebury Boulevard
Central Milton Keynes, MK9 2BE
www.authorhouse.co.uk
Phone: 08001974150

© 2009 Roger Carpenter. All rights reserved.

No part of this book may be reproduced, stored in a retrieval system, or transmitted by any means without the written permission of the author.

First published by AuthorHouse 3/17/2009

ISBN: 978-1-4389-3475-4 (sc)

Printed in the United States of America
Bloomington, Indiana

This book is printed on acid-free paper.

To James
Cross the Ocean
Best Wishes
Roger

This, the third book

in the Rutland series,

is for Audrey -

who is my everything.

Historical Characters you will meet in this book.

In order of appearance -

Colonel Sir Percy Wyndham
English eccentric, 1st New Jersey Cavalry

General George McClellan
General Commanding the Army of the Potomac

Captain John Reynolds
L Battery, 1st New York Regiment

General Joseph (Joe) Hooker
First Army Corps, Army of the Potomac

Lt Colonel Joshua Lawrence Chamberlain
20th Maine Infantry Regiment

General Winfield S Hancock
First Division, Army of the Potomac

General Henry J Hunt
Chief of Union Artillery, Army of the Potomac

Prologue

Major Arthur Rutland, Royal Artillery retired, stood at the porticoed doorway of his old Surrey farmhouse, Chellingham Place. He was formally dressed in a dark grey, long frock coat, and had a soft smile on his face as he looked across the paved courtyard towards the walled garden surrounding it. The bright summer sun shone directly down on the flowerbeds to make the whole scene glow vibrantly with colour. On this lovely June morning in 1900 he had a marvellous warm feeling of great pleasure deep inside him. He might even have admitted to almost having a smug satisfaction.

Though he was in his early eighties, he still had an erect stance; no longer the six foot four of his youth but he was still trim in shape. He had a head of white hair that, though thinning in places, matched his full moustache that cut across his tanned face. The reason for his feeling of great contentment was that this very day he was about to take Georgia, his daughter-in-law-to-be, by carriage to the local church, and there, as her father's representative, give her away to his own son, Peter.

Arthur felt a very deep affection for both Georgia and Peter, and he was certain that fate had thrown these two together for a happy future. Peter's previous, very happy marriage had been brought to a sudden and sad end by the tragic death of his wife Beatrice, who had sacrificed her life by visiting the poor in the East End of London as a doctor and there contracting cholera.

Then just recently, when Peter had served as a Lieutenant Colonel in the current Boer War in South Africa, the fates had smiled on him. While out there on active service, he had met Georgia, the American widow of an English cavalry Colonel. She was such a charming and vivacious young woman, who came from Vermont in New England.

Having accepted Peter's proposal of marriage, she had decided that she wanted to be married in an English country church there in Surrey, and then go back to the United States to visit her family with Peter.

So now Arthur was standing ready to take this young woman to the local village church and there, at her request, give her as a wife to his own son. There was nothing in the world that could have pleased him more.

Arthur's wife Millie and their daughter Tessa, and her children, had already gone to the church, so it was now just a matter of waiting until the landau carriage came to collect him and Georgia.

He looked towards the entrance gates as, with a clatter of hooves, the open-topped carriage, drawn by two greys, came into the courtyard and swung round to stand in front of the main door. Arthur turned and walked back inside the house to the long main hall that as usual was so delightfully cool from the summer heat.

"Georgia," he called. "The carriage is here." He heard a door upstairs open and close, and then came the sound of the rustling of a dress as Georgia slowly descended the stairs.

Arthur's heart rose to his mouth. She looked so stunningly beautiful in her ivory satin wedding dress that swept around her. Her exquisitely coiffured brown hair was set off with a headdress made of pearls and lily of the valley to emphasise her clear, fresh complexion and her large brown eyes. Arthur stepped forward to the foot of the stairs and held out his hand for her. "Come, my dear." It was easy to understand why his son had fallen in love with this beautiful young American and her soft New England voice.

As she reached the last step, Georgia reached out, took his hand and smiled at him. Arthur reached forward and gently squeezed her arm. He could not trust himself to speak. There was so much emotion and love welling up in him that he just might show too much feeling and then have a damp eye - that would never do.

He led her through the front hall and out into the bright sunlit courtyard. Holding her elbow he helped her mount the steps into the landau where she arranged the wedding dress around herself. With both Arthur and Georgia seated on the deep, leather, front-facing seat, the coachman gently tossed the reins on the horses' backs to walk the immaculately groomed greys out through the gates of the courtyard. They trotted down the approach lane from the farm and finally turned down the long, twisting country lane towards the local church.

Georgia turned her head to face Arthur and said. "When I'm married to Peter, what shall I call you? Major?"

"No, my dear, I think you should just call me Arthur."

"You are so sweet. That's very generous of you but I think I shall call you 'father' like my father back home, but just in case there is a mix-up I shall call you Father Rutland."

"That makes me sound rather like a parish priest."

"No one else will ever hear it but us in the family, and you and I will know who I mean, Father Rutland." She squeezed his hand and gave him a gentle kiss on his cheek.

St Leonard's was a typical small, spired, country church set on a hill with a line of old oaks bordering the approach lane. The landau stopped at the lychgate, where Arthur carefully assisted Georgia down from the steps, and then stood back as she adjusted her dress. He stepped forward and she took his arm to walk towards the church door where, ahead of them, the vicar and Arthur's three grandchildren were waiting as the two bridesmaids and the page.

The vicar led the way into the church while the organ played the beautiful and haunting Prince of Denmark's March. Arthur felt such great pride as he walked down the aisle towards the square-shouldered uniformed back of his son, who was waiting at the altar step. Arthur turned his head to the left where his wife was standing.

Rutland's Blues and Greys

He looked at her and she smiled in reply. Millie, his life long love. Millie, also with deep brown eyes. Millie, his everything. The memory of today, their son's wedding, would be one of the happiest days of their lives.

The vicar turned to them and started the service with "We are gathered here in the face of God to join these two people in holy matrimony."

It was three weeks later that Arthur and Millie were seated at the farmhouse dining table with Peter and Georgia who, in two days' time, were to travel to Southampton and start their voyage to America. During the dinner that evening, much of the conversation was about New England and the couple's forthcoming trip.

The pudding plates had been cleared and coffee was being drunk when Georgia said to Arthur, "Before Peter and I go back to America, I'd so like to hear about the time you spent there during the Civil War."

A silence fell across the table as Arthur lowered his head, put down his cup and wiped his moustache with his napkin. Millie looked along the length of the table at him and, after a pause, smiled and said softly, "Arthur, I think they should know all about it – before they go."

He nodded and, in silence, put down his napkin, pushed back his chair and stood up. He turned and slowly walked across the main hall towards his study. Peter looked at his mother and frowned a silent question at this rather strange behaviour. In reply she gently waved her hand to both him and Georgia, telling them to follow Arthur.

The two of them walked out of the dining room, crossed the hall and entered the study to see Arthur standing in front of the inglenook fireplace, his hand up on the large beam that ran over it, his foot resting on the long brass fender. He was looking down at the empty fireplace, obviously deep in thought.

Peter was at a loss to know what was happening, and also what to do. Georgia went up to Arthur, put her arm through his and said, "Father Rutland, if you'd rather not talk about it, we don't mind."

He turned to look at her, and into her deep brown eyes. He smiled, "No, my dear, I'll tell you my story. It's been a long time since I even thought about it but it's all coming back to me – and you'll have to make your own judgment at the end." Peter and Georgia glanced at each other in surprise at this unexpected comment.

Arthur picked up the home humidor, opened it and offered a cigar to his son. He turned round and looked at Georgia. "Do you mind if we smoke?" She smiled, then reached out and squeezed his arm in reply, appreciating his courtesy.

Arthur lit the bank of five candles in the wrought iron candelabra in the fireplace, to control the cigar smoke and help it up the empty chimney, and then lit his own cigar. He waved his arm for the two of them to sit in the other two easy chairs before he sat down in his own large leather, wingback chair. With the ashtray stand in easy reach beside him, he again looked in silence at the empty fireplace. Then he drew on his cigar, blew the smoke into the candle flame, and started his story.

"It was in mid-1862, when you Peter, and Tessa were just toddlers, that I received a telegram from Royal Artillery Headquarters in Woolwich. I was to report to Brigadier Sir David Chantler with all dispatch."

Chapter 1

On 17th July 1862, Major Arthur Rutland strode down the corridor on the first floor of the Royal Artillery Headquarters offices in Woolwich Barracks. His spurred boots made a sharp percussive sound as he marched along. He was in full dress uniform from his headgear of a busby with its scarlet bag on the right-hand side and the central white hackle, down to his shining boots. He was a very imposing figure in his dark blue Royal Artillery uniform; his height seemed to be emphasised by the red stripe down the outside of his trouser leg. His sword, controlled by his left hand, was held close to his leg. Medals, even with the ribbons firmly fixed, clinked on his chest to show he was a much travelled and very experienced gunner.

He scanned the name on each of the office doors that he passed until he saw 'Brigadier Sir David Chantler' on the shining brass nameboard. Arthur stopped, checked his uniform, and gently pulled the back of his jacket to ensure it was smooth under his sword belt.

He knocked, opened the door and walked in. A subaltern seated at the desk, rose and said, "How can I help, sir?"

"Major Rutland, to see Brigadier Chantler."

"Yes, sir, you are expected." The young officer knocked at the inner office door and went in. He quickly reappeared and held the door open. "Will you come through, sir?"

Arthur marched through the doorway and up to a large desk where the Brigadier sat. Arthur saluted, and Sir David got up from his seat.

"Afternoon, Major. Good to meet you." He was a large-framed man with a ruddy complexion and, at first glance, seemed to be of a friendly nature.

"Take a seat, Major." He gestured to a couple of large leather, high-back chairs to the side of the desk.

Arthur removed his busby and gave it to the subaltern, who said, "Shall I take your sword, sir?" Arthur lifted the sword and scabbard from the frog, gave it to the officer and he then sat down. During this time the Brigadier was looking at a bulky file on his desk.

"This is the file on 'Major Arthur Rutland', he said. "Well, Arthur, this is a damned big file with one hell of a lot of service in it. I've read through all of it and am very surprised at how far you've travelled in your career so far. Seeing all this makes me understand why the powers that be have chosen you for the posting I'm going to tell you about." He closed the file and said. "One thing I did notice was that you were in the Crimea in '55. In fact you were under the same Regimental Commander as myself. Did you know that?"

Arthur smiled. "Yes sir. I was a First Lieutenant, and most junior officers know who their commanders are but commanders cannot know all of their subordinates."

"Very politely said. Now tell me, Arthur. What do you know about America ?"

America ! Arthur was stunned. A posting in foreign parts, yes, but America !

"Um, do you mean America the continent or the United States of America ?"

"Damn it, I hadn't thought about the continent bit. No, I mean the United States of America, though they seem determined to tear themselves apart at the present moment."

"Well, sir, it's big."

"Ha! Damned right. Good start there."

"I think it is about the same size as Europe and I think I read that England will fit into their Great Lakes area."

"Will it, by God? Didn't know that. Now how about the economy and political state?"

Arthur was having to dig deep down into his memory as he had never had any real interest in the USA. His knowledge was just the bits picked up whilst reading the newspapers.

"With the economy part, the southern states are mainly agricultural, growing cotton and rice. They are based on a slave system that gives the labour force they need for the large areas of cropping. The north is industrialised and I expect the richer half."

He paused to gather together what information he could think of. Sir David did not interrupt. "The President of the northern USA is Abraham Lincoln, who is totally against the break-up of the Union. The President for the southern states, who I think call themselves a Confederation, is a President Davis. At present they seem to be having a terrible civil war with some victories but many unmitigated disasters on both sides." Again he paused. "I'm struggling now, sir. I might be able to think up a bit more but that nears my total knowledge of the USA."

"Well, in a geography exam you wouldn't do very well but you'd have beaten me." The Brigadier stood up and walked over to a big window that overlooked the large parade ground.

"You're right about the civil war, and that's the main item on our agenda." He turned to face Arthur. "Horse Guards, with Government approval, need to have observers out there to keep up with the type of fighting and how the Americans are handling it. We have a number of military attachés there with both sides but so far no one to represent the Royal Artillery."

He sat down at his desk again. "How do you feel about a posting there as an artillery observer and military attaché?"

"I'd be honoured by the offer but I hope I'd be with the Northern armies."

Sir David leaned forward and rested his elbows on the desk. "You might be surprised but a number of people fairly high up in our government think that the Northerners will lose and that the South will not only win the battles but will eventually dictate the political situation, certainly in the south and possibly most of America. As you said, it is a very big place. We can't understand the problems they have and the opportunities they can exploit." He looked down at his hands. "Yes, you will be with the Northern Army under Major General McClellan. I had to do a lot of hard work to get our sole observer there instead of with the South. Tell me, why do you want to be with the North?"

"I'd find it very difficult to be with men who condone slavery."

Sir David nodded. "I know what you mean, but there's no problem with that. You'll be with the North." He opened the file again. "You're in line for promotion to Lieutenant Colonel which will be gazetted shortly but you'll have a brevet rank of full Colonel in the field. It'll give you the status that you should have over there."

Arthur was delighted. "Thank you, sir I'm very impressed by the rank given to me."

"Arthur, you'll have a damned difficult path to follow. You must observe and report fully but only within the Americans' permissible limits, otherwise you might be accused of spying. You must not give advice, as this might be construed as a touch imperialistic but most important of all you must not become involved with any fighting whatsoever! That might mean you have to cut and run when others about you are fighting for their lives but you must not get involved." The Brigadier wagged his finger at Arthur to emphasise this point.

"All your reports can be examined by the American Army authorities if they wish but they should not ask you to delete or alter anything because the reports will be about your opinion of their methods – good or bad. They must not contain anything that might be of use to the Southern side, such as troop displacement or future movements. Do I make myself completely clear?"

"Certainly, sir."

"These reports will be delivered to the Legation in Washington for homeward passage, and they'll almost certainly end up on my desk. Any personal correspondence you want to send can be included with them, and I'll arrange for it to be passed on to whoever you wish." That was very good news to Arthur, for he was a great, and detailed, letter writer to his wife, Millie. She kept all his letters in strict date order from wherever he was in the world.

"On arrival in America you'll proceed to Washington and report to the British Ambassador, Lord Lyons, or his office. I'm not sure what kind of reception you'll receive as I don't know who Lyons sees as the victors, North or South. I trust he'll be as diplomatic about your posting as you will be in keeping him amiable. Now, have you any questions other than your transport arrangements?"

"How long is this posting likely to be for?"

"One, maybe two years. Would you like a posting for your wife as well?"

"No, thank you, sir, we have two children who should remain here with my wife."

"Subject to conditions I think we could arrange for leave after one year but that is very provisional because we've no idea of what the future holds for either side."

The Brigadier looked up at Arthur "That is all I can tell you right now. Anything extra that is available, I'll let you have before you sail."

"When exactly is that, sir?"

Sir David pulled over a wallet file and said, "You are to sail on 19th August in the RMS Scotia from

Liverpool." He closed the file and handed it over the desk to Arthur, who took it and stood up. The Brigadier also stood up and offered his hand to Arthur. "I think you have a very tough task ahead of you, Colonel. All the best."

"Thank you, sir." Arthur shook the Brigadier's hand, drew himself to attention then turned and walked back into the outer office.

....

On 18th August 1862, after a long and tedious train journey from London, Arthur arrived at Liverpool's main station on Lime Street. A uniformed travel agent had arranged a cab for him and ensured all his luggage was loaded.

"Your ship is in the Huskisson Dock on Regent Road, sir," said the agent. "Your cabbie will show you where you are to check in."

Arthur thanked the man and climbed into the cab. It was a three-mile trip from the centre of Liverpool out to the dock area, which proved to be a hive of activity. All the goods of the world were being unloaded from ships and then replaced with all the British goods destined for export around the world. As he passed the docks' entrances he was amused by the names over the gates – Trafalgar, Nelson, and Wellington.

At last he saw the sign for the Huskisson Dock. The cab moved up to the main sheds during which time Arthur tried to remember a military Huskisson. The cabbie reined in and a Cunard official came to the cab. "Your name, please, sir?"

Arthur gave his details and the Cunard official instructed two lascar porters to take Arthur's cases to the sheds.

"Huskisson," said Arthur to the Cunard man. "Who was he?"

The official smiled. "Some bigwig politician from years ago but best known as the first man to be killed in a railway accident." Arthur also smiled at this tenuous claim to fame and followed the official to the main sheds.

He entered the passenger departure area, presented his tickets and had his baggage taken for loading. Then he went out onto the actual Huskisson Dock on Merseyside to board the ship. As he left the cover of the departure sheds, he saw for the first time the amazing sight of the Royal Mail Steamer ' Scotia '. She was the pride of the Cunard Line, and had only recently completed her very successful maiden voyage to America in May. To Arthur's eyes she was enormous, with her full length of almost 900 feet, and fitted on either side with massive paddle wheels over 40 feet in diameter which were driven by 1000 horsepower engines. From the elegant figurehead protruding from the bows right back to the rakish stern, she looked exactly what she was, an elegant floating hotel. Apparently she could carry up to 500 First Class Passengers, who could be dined, 300 at a time, in sumptuous surroundings.

Arthur stood on the quay side for some time just looking up at the beautiful lines of this amazing ship. He had sailed on a number of military transport ships in his time, but he had never been transported in such luxury. He smiled to himself and thought, 'I'm going to enjoy my nine day voyage – at the Army's expense.'

His main trunks, and baggage that was not wanted on voyage, had already been taken on board and put into the hold below decks. Even the personal suitcase and grip holding the clothing he needed for the voyage were both already placed in his cabin, Number 149. He had been surprised at the high number of his cabin but he had learned that there were in fact just over 250 cabins though not all were full as there were only 396 passengers travelling on board. The cuisine was supposed to equal the quality of the most noted hotels in the Kingdom. He was certain that, when he eventually arrived in America and joined up with the Northern Army, he would certainly be living in most uncomfortable conditions with very basic food, but at least until then he would be travelling in style.

That evening Arthur, dressed in his blue mess jacket and trousers plus a scarlet waistcoat, entered the dining room. It was an amazing sight with its curved timbered ceiling like the inside of a clinker-built boat, above him. The whole room glistened and shone. The light source came from gimballed oil lamps fixed to the walls and to the main columns. These gave a warm golden light which was reflected from the silver cutlery and cut-glass tableware.

The head steward stood just inside the dining room with a list of the passengers' details on a lectern. Arthur gave his cabin number and asked if he could have a single table.

"Certainly, sir, if you'll follow me," said the steward, who then started to weave his way between a number of tables with Arthur following a few steps behind.

As the steward passed a table where a lady and gentleman were seated, the lady's silver evening bag fell onto the floor. Arthur bent down and picked it up. He offered it to the lady and said, "Your bag, madam."

The lady said with a smile, "Oh, thank you so much. I would have missed that greatly." She took the bag and Arthur turned to follow the steward, who was now some way ahead, when he heard a voice from behind him call out. "Excuse me, ah, General." Arthur paused but he did not turn round; the call must have been for someone else.

"Ah, General I wonder if you would…"

Arthur realised that the voice was addressing him. He turned to see that the gentleman from the table with the lady was standing up and looking at him. The man was tall and slim with sandy coloured hair worn long almost down to his shoulders, and was impeccably dressed in a black frock coat with a silver waistcoat. At his throat he had a bright yellow and blue striped cravat.

"I beg your pardon, did you mean me?" asked Arthur.

"Yes, sir," replied the man. "My wife wondered if you would care to join us for dinner?" Arthur stood amazed and even felt nonplussed. How extraordinary, he thought. But the man's voice was certainly American so maybe this was not such an abnormal happening for him.

Rutland's Blues and Greys

"Well, that's very kind of you, sir, but I don't think I can impose myself on you like...."

"No, no, General, it would be our pleasure, especially my wife's." That comment put Arthur in a different, if not difficult, position. He could brazen it out with a man, but when a lady requested his company that could not be refused with any decorum.

Arthur looked at the lady. She was in her forties and very attractive. She had light brown hair piled on her head into a swirled coiffured knot. Her high-necked dress was coffee coloured with a pearl necklace around her throat – it all suited her perfectly. She smiled, and it was that smile that Arthur knew he could not refuse.

"If you are sure that…" he started.

"Oh, most certainly," she said. "Please sit down here," she gestured to a seat at the table that was already set for a third person.

"This is very good of you to dine with us, General," said the man.

Arthur nodded his acknowledgement. "I hope I don't disappoint you, sir, but I am not a General, merely a Colonel in Her Majesty's Royal Artillery."

"There you are, Abigail. Didn't I say he was an English Army officer?"

Arthur smiled and, giving a slight bow, said to the lady, "I am Arthur Rutland, at your service, ma'am."

She smiled back and held up her hand, which Arthur gently took. He pulled out the chair and sat down at the table.

"I'm sorry, Colonel," said the man. "I'm Hiram J. Eaves, and this is my wife Abigail. My wife saw you as you came up the gangplank boarding the ship and said to me that she'd like to meet you as you'd be so very interesting.

"Hiram, you are so indiscreet." Abigail exclaimed. Arthur noted that her accent was softer than her husband's. 'Was this the Southern accent he had been told about? Hiram from his harder voice was surely a Northerner, possibly a New Yorker,' he thought.

"Madam, you share the same interest as myself, watching people, and possibly wondering what they do?" Arthur asked.

"Yes, exactly. I love to sit and watch passers-by and, just as you say, wonder where they come from, why they are here. It's such fun." She put her napkin to her lips and said. "We've been in England for the past four months and I simply adore your courtesy and tradition of good manners. It may seem a little quaint to us pushy Americans but I loved being in amongst your quality of life. When I saw you coming on board, I felt I had to talk to you. You were my last chance to enjoy the glamour of England."

"You flatter me, ma'am. I'm just a soldier. Nothing more, nothing less."

"There, you have just proved what I have said to be absolutely correct," she replied. Arthur frowned at her comment."

"You are a Colonel, a person of standing, yet, Arthur, you say you're just a soldier. May I call you Arthur?"

"Most certainly."

"Then you must call me Abigail." Arthur smiled an acknowledgement.

"My God," interjected Hiram. "The Colonel here was hoping for a quiet meal and you aren't giving him any peace."

Arthur turned to face Hiram and said. "Hiram, I think it might be easier for the general discussion if you called me Arthur rather than Colonel. I feel we might get rather mixed up otherwise."

The couple laughed at this comment as the steward came up to take their order. When this was completed, Arthur asked Abigail, "Where have you been in England?"

"Hiram came over here on business so we've been to the Midlands, I think you call it, to see the factories he wanted and then we came down to London and travelled into Surrey and Kent. We stayed at country houses and large hotels and simply soaked up the luxurious atmosphere."

"Were you able to see the apple blossom in Kent?"

"Oh yes. Our agent took us for a long carriage drive through the orchards; it was all so beautiful. Where do you come from, Arthur?"

"I live in a small village called Chellingham on the North Downs."

"The Downs, is that a flat area?"

"No, it is a typical English expression. The Downs are a range of hills. They are not very high, just about 800 feet at the highest."

"And why are you going to America?"

Arthur paused. He was not expecting to be asked that question by a non-military person, so speaking with careful thought, he said. "I'm a military attaché going to the British Legation in Washington."

"To observe our civil war?" asked Hiram.

"Yes." He said. "It sounds macabre for a Government to send observers to a field of battle where men are dying but we all have to learn our trade by watching how others do it."

Hiram nodded. "Strange you should say that, Arthur, because that is exactly what I've been doing over the past few weeks."

The wine waiter appeared at Hiram's elbow with a bottle of white wine. Hiram tasted it and accepted it. The waiter served Abigail and then Arthur before he filled Hiram's glass and then, having placed the bottle in a chill bucket, he left.

Hiram lifted his glass and said. "A toast to my clever lady wife, and to England." Glasses were raised and the toast was drunk. Arthur wondered about the toast to Abigail but naturally did not comment.

There was a pause as Hiram put his glass down, then he looked at Abigail and smiled. "You are right as always, my dear. The English have the perfect manners." Arthur was at a complete loss as to the toast and the comment.

Hiram looked at him and said, "I think that all of my friends, and any new acquaintance in America, would have said after my toast, 'why is your wife clever?'- but you, sir, did not flinch. Well done, Arthur." Arthur, who felt as though he was being put to some sort of test, remained silent but attentive.

Hiram leaned forward on the table. "I have a large and very prosperous leather footwear factory just outside Boston, Massachusetts. It's been in the family for many years and has grown on quality and the range of goods. For some time I've felt there must be newer and better ways of stitching the leatherwork of shoes and bootees, and at last we found the McKay machine. This has been a great step forward." He paused to sip his wine.

"Hiram," said Abigail, "are you sure Arthur wants to hear all this?" Before Arthur could reply, Hiram said, "I'm sure he will when I've finished." Hiram looked at Arthur, "My lady wife said we should go to England to find out the latest way that the English are handling the new machines." Hiram leaned back in his chair. "This clever little lady was absolutely correct and at the same time we've both met and learned to like the English and your way of life."

Arthur raised his glass and said, "And I am looking forward to learning about America and your way of life."

Chapter 2

The eight days that it took them to cross the Atlantic were very enjoyable, though occasionally the large ship rolled enough to send a number of the passengers to their cabins, and away from the dining room, but by and large, the journey was in pleasant weather.

Arthur met Abigail and Hiram either at meals or in the main lounge where they often talked for a long time. The Eaves wanted to know more of England and about Arthur, while he questioned them about what he would find when he arrived in Washington.

One afternoon Abigail and Hiram were seated on a settee with Arthur sitting in a large club chair opposite them when Abigail said, "Arthur, it's obvious that you have travelled a great deal in your career. How did you mange to find time to meet and marry your wife?" Arthur threw back his head and gave a laugh.

"On one leave from India," he said. "I was on a pheasant shoot in Kent on the land owned by a Mr John Martin. At the shoot lunch I met his daughter, who was called Amelia but everyone called her Millie, and I fell

Rutland's Blues and Greys

in love on the spot in the proverbial manner. I courted her and found that she loved me so I asked her father for her hand. He wasn't very happy at first because I was stationed abroad but Millie would not be gainsaid, so we married after a whirlwind courtship of only three months."

"Well, I do declare," exclaimed Abigail. "That is so quick."

"My goodness, you guys really move fast," said Hiram. "But then I guess that's just the difference between you impetuous, romantic English and us staid, laconic Americans. We just keep everything bottled up inside as we gaze into the far distances of the West, chewing our tobacco and worrying about the next Indian attack." Arthur smiled at Hiram's witticism and felt the warmth of mutual appreciation for him.

"You said that you have two sons? What do they do?" asked Arthur. Abigail and Hiram exchanged glances before Hiram replied. "Casey the younger of the two is in the Union Navy with Admiral Farragut. Hopefully he is well."

Arthur suddenly had the horrible thought that maybe the other son was fighting for the Confederates. Surely that was not possible.

"Carter, the older one runs my factory. He was badly wounded in the legs at the Battle of Balls Bluff in '61. He finds it very difficult to get about but his legs are slowly improving and we hope they'll be almost perfect eventually."

"I'm so sorry to hear about his injuries," said Arthur.

"There is one good part to him coming to work at the factory," said Hiram. "He told me that the quality of the bootees supplied to the Army was terrible. Poor quality at high prices."

Hiram leaned forward and tapped Arthur on the knee. "Do you know I had to actually bribe an official to take a sample of my shoes to the War Department? If I hadn't, they would have gone on buying rubbish. I sell all my bootees to the army at cost price plus 20 cents profit per pair. That undercuts even the worst quality product, but, because it is a guaranteed market, even at that very low price I'm making a great deal of money."

"You say bootees?" asked Arthur.

"Oh yes, you call them boots but to us that means the tall knee-length boots used by the cavalry."

"And then there's my brother," said Abigail.

Arthur frowned at the comment – it sounded as though she did not approve of her brother's actions.

Abigail paused and looked at her hands. "You might have noticed from my voice, that I am from the South. My family, the La Trobes, live in Georgia. My brother Jonathan is an officer in the Confederate Cavalry." Again she paused. "I'm so glad that it is now impossible for him and our son to fight against each other." Almost in a whisper to herself, she added, "A civil war is such a terrible thing."

Hiram changed the subject by saying, "Where will you be staying when you reach Washington, Arthur?"

"I don't know."

"At the present we've a house near Boston but Carter is taking that over with his wife," said Hiram. "Shortly

Rutland's Blues and Greys

we're moving into my old family house that my parents had in Baltimore. My mother died some time ago while my father died just last year. We're going to renovate the family home and live there. I've a brother who also lives in Baltimore too. He's a doctor. He's married and has two sons. Thankfully they're too young to fight."

Hiram looked at Abigail and then turning back to Arthur, said, "If you are ever in the area, please write us and we would love for you to stay."

Arthur looked up at these two generous people and said, "You're so kind. I am little boy lost in your big country but having you as friends means a great deal to me, and, yes, I will contact you if it at all possible, to meet you again. Thank you so much for your offer."

"I'll give you a copy of the address later on." .

That evening Arthur had a last dinner with Hiram and Abigail.

"Oh, Arthur," said Abigail, and put her hand on his arm. "I'm so going to miss these lovely dinners with you when we get home."

"Abigail, the past week has been such a very enjoyable time for me. Your conversation and your beauty have made this a journey of a lifetime for me."

Abigail gently slapped him on the arm with her folded fan. "Oh fiddle de dee. Now stop it, you flatterer."

"No, Abigail," said Arthur. "I am serious. I was expecting good food and a comfortable cabin on this trip but to have met you both has been a great joy for me. I have learned so much from our talks and the time has simply flown by. I am so grateful to you both."

He reached across to hold her hand and said, "If I was not deeply in love with my wife, and you were not married, I would certainly have been courting you. You are a beautiful and very exciting lady."

"Oh, Arthur!" she exclaimed, flipping open her fan to hide her face, which was blushing at the obviously sincere compliments.

Arthur turned to Hiram. "And as for you, sir," he said. "Seriously I'm so indebted to you for your information that you've given to me of what I can expect to find in America."

"The feeling is absolutely mutual," said Hiram. "We've so enjoyed your company also. I do hope that we can meet again. I feel that though we are of different nationalities and cultures, we have such a great deal in common."

Arthur lifted his glass. "May I propose a toast to the two great Uniteds. The United States of America and the United Kingdom." Three glasses were raised to the toast.

"You will come and visit us in the fall, won't you, Arthur?" said Abigail with longing in her eyes.

"It is a certainty," replied Arthur.

That evening, seated at his desk in his cabin, Arthur wrote his usual letter to Millie and said that though he had always prepared himself before he went to a new posting by finding out about the life and the language, he had automatically thought that with America it would be similar to Great Britain even rather colonial. He said that he was right in that courtesy and friendship applied, but he was wrong in many other aspects and that he had great deal to learn.

After eight days at sea, the Cunard liner 'Scotia' slowly eased her way up the Hudson River towards New

Rutland's Blues and Greys

York. Eventually the liner slipped into her berth at Pier 40, North River, at the end of a crazy-looking array of wharves that, though presumably efficient, seemed very dated and due for improvement.

Having said his farewells to the Eaves, he eventually disembarked and was met on the quayside by an agent from the Legation, who told him that he and his luggage were booked on a train on the first leg of the journey to Washington. The train would leave in four hours' time from the main Baltimore and Ohio station using the Consolidated Railways of New Jersey. Of the three railroads used, it would be the Philadelphia, Wilmington and Baltimore Railway that would eventually bring him into the station at Washington.

Though all in first class coaches, the 13-hour journey was very tiring despite passing through interesting and at times beautiful countryside.

He had been informed that he was booked into Kirkwood House Hotel on Pennsylvania Avenue and 12th Street in Washington, so having loaded his baggage into a cab which had taken him from the Baltimore & Ohio Station, he was carried to the hotel. On checking into the hotel, he was given a note from the Legation by the hotel reception clerk, requesting that he should see a Mr Michael Barrington at 10.30 am the next day. The British Legation had done very efficient work in organising his travel arrangements and his hotel booking.

Next morning he hired a cab from outside the Hotel and instructed the driver to take him to the British Legation on H Street. It only took a few minutes but when he arrived, Arthur was amazed to see that the official building of Her Majesty's Ambassador to the United States of America was a very large and imposing family house that, incredibly, was painted completely black! Black woodwork, ironwork and even the bricks - all black! The cab stopped at the entrance gate and a uniformed doorman opened the cab door and held it.

"Is this the British Legation?" asked Arthur in amazement as he got out.

"Yes, sir," replied the doorman.

"But why is it all painted black?"

"The Ambassador did it to show we are nothing to do with the American President's White House just up the road."

"Really?" queried Arthur.

"Really, sir."

Arthur took some coins out of his pocket and showed them to the doorman. "Take what is necessary to pay the cabbie with a tip, please," he said. The doorman sorted through them and gave some change to the driver.

Arthur walked through the large front door of the British Legation from H Street. In the entrance hall was a clerk seated at a desk. Arthur walked up to him and said, "I am Colonel Rutland to see Mr Barrington."

The clerk gestured to a line of chairs. "If you will take a seat, sir, I will inform Mr Barrington that you are here." Arthur walked over to the chairs and sat down. The clerk called over a messenger and gave him a handwritten note.

After a few minutes the man returned to the clerk who stood up and came over to Arthur.

"Mr Barrington is able to see you now, sir," he said. "The messenger will show you the way."

Rutland's Blues and Greys

Arthur followed the messenger along a marble floored corridor to a large polished door where the messenger knocked and opened the door for Arthur to walk in. A clerk seated at a desk got up and said, "Colonel Rutland?" Arthur nodded and the clerk walked over to an internal door. He tapped on it and then opened it. "Colonel Rutland, sir," he announced and stood to one side.

Arthur walked through the doorway and into the room to see a slim, fair-headed man seated behind a desk. The man stood up. "Colonel Rutland, pleased to see you. I am Michael Barrington. Please take a seat."

"Thank you," replied Arthur.

"I'm one of Lord Lyons' aides and I'm instructed to assist you on your arrival." He picked up a file and opened it. "I am not sure whether you will be attached to the Army of the Potomac or of Virginia. I have here letters of introduction and authorisation for either one." He turned the pages. "Now here is your accommodation address. This will be available for you during all of your time in America even while you are actually with the army. I'll have a messenger show you the way there." He closed the file and said, "Is there anything else I can do for you, Colonel?"

"Most certainly. I would like your advice and information on meeting and mixing with the Americans. Your comments on the civil war and what I should see and do here, plus any words of wisdom that you have learned while being here and you feel I would benefit from."

"Well, well," said Barrington leaning back in his chair. "Normally the moment I've given details of living accommodation to any visiting British official, they're off to tell the Yanks how they should act to be half as good as us English. Colonel, I warm to you."

Arthur smiled at the comment. "I think that I'll be seeking your advice often in the future and so perhaps you'll call me Arthur."

Barrington reached his hand out across the desk "With pleasure, Arthur. My name is Michael." He sat down again and then said, "I know the very man you should meet." He picked up a small handbell on his desk and rang it to call in the outside clerk.

"Matthew, will you please go and find Colonel Sir Percy Wyndham? He was in the Legation earlier and is possibly still here. Please give him my compliments and ask him if he would be so kind as to come to my office as I have someone who would be interested in meeting him."

"Very good, sir," said Matthew and left the office.

Barrington rested his elbows on the desk and said to Arthur, "Colonel Wyndham is a most remarkable man. He is about to return to his regiment. I hope I can get him to meet you and I'm sure he will be a font of knowledge for you especially on military matters."

Within a minute Matthew returned and said, "I'm afraid, sir, that Colonel Wyndham has left the office and presumably has left the Legation."

"That's a shame but I hope you will bump into him at some time. He is an amazing man. Let me think now." Barrington leaned back in his chair and stared at the ceiling. He was trying to remember all the details.

"Sir Percy Wyndham. He has served in the French Army and Navy. He then returned to England and served in the Royal Artillery. Later he joined the Austrian Cavalry and then fought under Garibaldi in Sicily. He was knighted by King Victor Emmanuel."

Barrington looked at Arthur. "Impressed?"

"Very," replied Arthur.

"He then offered his services to the Union. General McClellan had heard of him and arranged for him to command the 1st New Jersey Cavalry, a volunteer regiment. He trained them to be a very efficient regiment until disaster struck."

"Disaster?" queried Arthur.

"Yes. In June his regiment ran into an ambush south of Harrisonburg and in a sharp skirmish he was captured but as luck would have it, he has just been paroled and is right now returning to the 1st New Jersey." Barrington paused again. "It's a shame you didn't meet him. I'm sure he would be of great help to you with your queries on all matters to do with the Union military."

He picked up a sheet of paper from the file. "Look, here are the details of your lodging in G Street, where you have rooms in a boarding house. As soon as I know where Colonel Wyndham is, I'll contact you and him."

Arthur, realising that the meeting was over, stood up and picked up his busby. "Thank you very much for you assistance, Michael."

"Not at all. If you don't meet up with Sir Percy, come and see me again and I'll give you what background information I can. If I can be of any assistance at any other time, just call in. Oh, by the way, you might see Sir Percy on the street. He is very easy to recognise as he has thick black hair and also a ten-inch long moustache. He wears high cavalry boots and a plumed slouch hat."

"My goodness," said Arthur. "He would certainly stand out in a crowd."

"I think you might find a number of officers similarly attired in Washington," commented Barrington. "But not many wearing a busby with scarlet side bag."

Arthur laughed. "I take your point."

In the Legation main hall, just before he reached the outer door, Arthur stopped to put on his busby, making sure that the scarlet bag was hanging straight. From behind him he heard a loud, clear, English-sounding voice call out. "A British Colonel, Cavalry or Artillery, I think."

Arthur turned to see an upright, well-built, bright-faced man with a enormously large bushy black moustache spreading right across his face and overlapping his cheeks, while a thick mass of black hair covered his head.

Arthur saw that he wore the silver eagle on his shoulder boards, denoting a Union Colonel, and he deduced that this must be the very Colonel Wyndham that Barrington was hoping he would meet.

"Royal Artillery, Sir Percy."

"Ha!" laughed Wyndham. "Now you have me at a disadvantage, sir."

"Colonel Arthur Rutland."

"Well, I'll be damned," said Sir Percy "Yours is the first English voice I've heard apart from this Legation for months.

"Actually, I have just seen Mr Barrington, who recommended that I try and contact you."

"Why's that, my dear chap?"

"I'm a new boy in America, and at the game of military attaché. I asked Barrington for advice and he recommended you as the best source of military wisdom."

"My God, Arthur, you have a fine turn of phrase. I can't refuse your request. Now, have you had lunch?" asked Sir Percy.

"I haven't had breakfast yet," Arthur replied

"My goodness, you'll simply fade away. In Washington the Yanks eat like horses."

He had put on his slouch hat and led Arthur from the 'Black House'. "Their normal breakfast," he said, "is fried oysters followed by a large steak and to finish, a blancmange. As for me, for lunch I shall expect stuffed flounder and some crab cakes followed by game pie and ending with a buttermilk pie. Keeps the figure rounded, what!"

Outside, as they walked along the sidewalk, Sir Percy continued his description. "After a decent lunch, they go rather strange. They have dinner at about 5 o'clock followed by a good sized 'tea' at 7.30, often followed by a supper at nine. God knows where they put it all. Even I can't manage all that, but a lot of 'em do."

He strode down H Street towards Pennsylvania Avenue. "Now be my guest and let me take you to Willard's City Hotel, run by the Willard brothers who have the best food in Washington – and the sweetest water from their very own well."

So, over an enormous lunch, Arthur was introduced, by a larger-than-life English eccentric, to the inside knowledge of Washington from the epicurean to the political, from the military to the seamy. Wyndham surprised Arthur by telling him that he should wear his sword and revolver most of the time. He warned that what with Johnny Reb likely to turn up anywhere, plus Union deserters around in the country and dark streets in any town, it was essential always to be armed.

Sir Percy sipped his coffee and then wiped a napkin across his enormous moustache.

"I've been talking too damned much but I'll summarise it all into this." He drew at his large cigar and said, "There are just as many rogues here as in London but they might well appear different. The Federal Army has some damned fine generals and some pathetic ones, with the right ones not always at the top. And finally, if you want to see the real Union Army and how good the men are, then attach yourself to one or two batteries and stick with them. You'll find they are completely different from the regular soldiers that you and I know in Britain. They're not as strictly disciplined as ours but by God, when properly trained, they fight like heroes because they believe in what they are fighting for."

Eventually outside Willard's, as they were about to part, Sir Percy said, "One last piece of personal advice, Arthur, I would suggest that you don't wear your busby. Have a British Staff peaked cap or even a Union Army blue cap with your own badge on it." He paused. "Maybe you could wear a large slouch hat like mine but not bigger, otherwise I'll be annoyed." With mutual laughter and a shaking of hands, the two men went their separate ways.

Rutland's Blues and Greys

Arthur left his meeting with Colonel Sir Percy Wyndham with his head buzzing and his stomach full to bursting. Back at his hotel he arranged for all his kit to be moved to the rooming house in 14th Street between G and H Street, only a couple of hundred yards from the British Legation.

Eventually inside the sitting room of this compact town house, he carefully placed his busby on its stand and unpacked his field staff peaked cap. This was flat topped and round, with four-inch sides that were embellished with a red three-inch band, plus a peak with gold braid on the edge. It would be entirely different from the Union Army Cap but not as flamboyant as the busby.

It was well into the evening when with all his other kit finally organised and stored away, he slumped into an easy chair and made a decision. He would not eat anything more that day and he would go to bed.

Next morning, having found a small eating house, he had some coffee and rolls. Then, as suggested by Sir Percy, he walked along 14th Street and made his way to the War Department, which was next to the White House, to find out where he could catch up with the Federal forces.

The answer to this was the Army of the Potomac, but he was told that it would take some time before he could be permitted to actually join the staff as there was a great deal of activity and change going on. It was then suggested that while he waited he might like to spend some time looking around the city.

He started by seeing Barrington at the Legation again, who gave him introductions to a number of people in the Legation and in the city who would be of use or interest to him.

Then, for the next few days he did a tourist trail around the city. He walked down close to the Potomac to see the unfinished Washington Memorial, which apparently was going to be a large spire or column but at present was just a stump of hewn stone blocks set in a muddy field and surrounded by cattle.

He walked down Pennsylvania Avenue towards the Capitol Building which did not look a great deal better. Though a lot of the actual building was well advanced, the large dome was still just a framework, but many workmen could be seen all over the huge site. Arthur was told that the President had insisted that the dome should be completed even though the Union was at war because it would show his confidence in the future.

The tour was not the pleasure that he expected it would be as the whole of Washington was a hive of activity with Army wagons streaming through the city and churning up dust or mud on the very basic roads. The drivers of the wagons were continually shouting and swearing at other road users to clear the way - while the stink from open drains was everywhere.

After a few days, news of the defeat of General Pope's Army of Virginia started coming in. Apparently General John Pope, an arrogant, incompetent and self-opinionated man, had just been given a bloody nose at the Second Battle of Bull Run.

Eventually Arthur learned that this Army of Virginia had retired towards Washington and was now being reformed and added to the Army of the Potomac under General McClellan, who was to bring it all back into a fighting force.

General Robert E Lee, the Commander of the Confederate Army of Northern Virginia, was now within striking distance of Washington, and all the citizens of Washington were in a great state of panic. In utter desperation, Lincoln had reinstated General McClellan, the very man who he had fired just a few months before because he seemed to have no drive. But regardless of his faults or timidity, McClellan was an excellent organiser and it was he who would command the joint Armies of Virginia and of the Potomac, and get them back into fighting trim again. This joint Army was now based at Rockville in Maryland just 30 miles north-west of Washington.

When Arthur heard the name McClellan, it rang a bell with him somewhere back in his past.

'McClellan.' Arthur dug back into his memory for his recollection of the name that he felt he had heard of a long time ago. Then it came to him. When he was outside Sevastopol in the Crimea, there was an American military observer named McClellan. He wondered if it was the same man.

Chapter 3

Confederate General Lee was in a great dilemma. Though he had won a number of victories, his Army of Northern Virginia was now numerically greatly reduced through exhaustion, sickness, starvation and exposure, to around 50,000 men. Because of the lack of all materiel, from boots to ammunition, from feed to fodder, it was in very poor condition. Lee was certain he would not able to attack Washington directly, especially as it was reported that McClellan was about to receive 60,000 replacements as an immediate response to Lincoln's call for 300,000 more men. Nor could he keep his men where they were. He had to move them on to obtain provisions. It was politically impossible for him to drop back into Virginia so, regardless of all risks, he had to take his army north across the Potomac River. Lee now felt confident enough to take the war to the North by marching into Maryland. It was there that he intended to put pressure on the shattered Union Army as they would have to follow him, and in doing

Rutland's Blues and Greys

so they would leave his home state of Virginia free from occupation.

He certainly gained with this move because he would be able to feed his hungry army from the rich stores and farmland of Maryland. He also hoped that by this show of strength Maryland, as yet undecided which side to support, might then move to throw its weight behind the South. This extra support for the Confederacy could well mean that the pressure on the North to end the war would become overwhelming.

Lee also felt that a major victory in the North could well ensure recognition for the South from Europe, and might even bring Britain and France to give them aid and recognition, so he marched his ragged army of men into Maryland. Because thousands of her sons were already fighting with the Confederate North Virginian Army, it was expected that thousands more would flock to the colours after the recent victories.

He used White Ferry, twenty miles south of Frederick, as a crossing point of the Potomac where his Army of Northern Virginia could wade across the clear and placid water. As they crossed, the sounds of a new, year-old song could be heard being played by the regimental bands, 'Maryland, My Maryland'. This had been written to commemorate the clash between Federal troops and Southern sympathisers in Baltimore.

On September 5th, for the first time, the Confederate army was on Union land. Because Maryland was counted as a Southern slave state, all the men of the Confederate Army of Northern Virginia were under strict instructions not to pillage for food or clothing and had been told to pay for all their requirements. But it soon became obvious that the local inhabitants had no sympathy for Lee's army.

Then Lee took an amazing and a very bold action. He decided to split his forces and send General 'Stonewall' Jackson with 22,000 men, almost half his army, to capture the Union strong point of Harper's Ferry to the south-west and take all its stores, while Lee himself would continue his advance to the north. Harper's Ferry was not only a Federal garrison of 13,000 men but it was also an arsenal rich in stores of weapons and clothing.

Lee was confident that after their defeat at Manassas, the Federal Generals Pope or McClellan could not possibly reorganise the Federal Army of the Potomac for some weeks. Lee decided that the remainder of his own army would pierce deep into Pennsylvania and eventually reunite with Jackson. He made this split of his army in the face of the Union Army because he was certain that McClellan, though with an army probably twice the size of Lee's, would be slow and lack the courage to take the initiative.

But McClellan had only needed a few days to get his army into fighting order again and swiftly he moved it westwards. By 7th September he had moved his headquarters out of Washington to Rockville, Maryland. When Lee discovered this, he realised that with his army split, he was in danger of being defeated in detail.

On 8th September Arthur reported to McClellan's headquarters in Rockville's town centre and gave his letter of authority to the General's Aide de Camp.

After a short wait, a Captain led him down the corridor and opened the door to the General's office.

Rutland's Blues and Greys

Arthur walked smartly in to see that General McClellan was seated at a table across the room with a number of men standing around.

"Come in, Colonel," called the General.

Arthur strode across to the table, halted and threw a crisp salute that General McClellan returned.

"At ease, Colonel," said McClellan and looked down at Arthur's papers. "I see from these details that you were in the Crimea."

"Yes, sir, at about the same time that you were there."

"Well, I learned a great deal of interest while I was there." The General stopped and looked at Arthur, as though he was expecting a response to his comment.

"I expect, sir," said Arthur, "that one of the main facts you learned was that we had the most crassly inefficient supply and support system. And I suspect, sir, you were amazed that we actually won."

McClellan leaned back in his chair and looking carefully at Arthur said, "And despite the bad supply system, Colonel, how did you win?"

Having led the conversation into the subject, Arthur replied with confidence. "Through the steadfastness and good training of the British infantry, supported by superior artillery."

"And has the British Army learned the lesson you have just mentioned?"

"I hope so, sir. We're rather slow to change but the terrible cost of the victory in the Crimea showed that we had to become more efficient."

"Colonel," said McClellan. "I have created a well-trained army which is about to be used against the rebels. Recently we've had a setback but we are now hot on the trail of General Lee, and I think you'll be seeing a battle fairly soon. Are you here to teach us how best to use our cannon?"

"No, sir. I'm here to learn how you use them to the best advantage."

General McClellan smiled. "I think you're a bit of a diplomat as well as a soldier." He folded up Arthur's papers and handed them back. "Colonel, you are free to go wherever you wish. I'll inform my Generals that they are to give you every assistance that you request."

"That is most generous of you, sir. I'll try not to be a burden to them."

"Please dine with my staff. I'll instruct my Generals to make you welcome."

Arthur saluted, turned on his heel and left the room.

As Arthur left the HQ building, he saw an officer standing by a desk near the entrance talking to a sergeant who was seated at it. The officer appeared to be connected to the Provost HQ security.

Arthur looked at his shoulder boards and saw two golden leaves. "Excuse me, Major, could you assist me?"

The officer looked at Arthur, then at his uniform, and he was obviously unsure who Arthur was, or his rank.

Arthur continued. "I'm Colonel Rutland, a British officer in the Royal Artillery, and a military attaché to General McClellan's staff." Instantly the Major came to attention and saluted, "Certainly, sir. How can I help?"

Arthur returned the salute. "I've just arrived here and have seen the General but now I'm wanting to visit the artillery park and meet up with some of the batteries."

"Let's see," said the Major and picked up a sheet of paper from the desk. "Ah yes. If you turn right down the main road north towards Gaithersburg, and keep on for about one mile there you will start to see gun parks. I think that one of the first batteries will be the 1st New York Light, though I am sure if you ask for the commander of any of the batteries there, they'll be able to help you."

"Thank you, Major," replied Arthur.

"Has your lodging been arranged for you, sir?"

"No, not yet. The General said that I'd be cared for by the staff of any corps I chose. I wanted to acquaint myself with the artillery first."

The Major smiled. "I think you might have that wrong, sir. You'll be more comfortable with the staff than with the guns. With all due respect, sir, I think the batteries would prefer if you lodged with the staff rather than them."

Arthur laughed. "Very diplomatic, Major. Find my lodgings - then find the guns."

"Excuse me a moment, sir," said the Major and walked over to a door. He entered and closed the door behind him. After a couple of minutes he reappeared.

"I have your details now, sir and I've arranged your lodgings." He handed a sheet of paper to Arthur. "I've taken the liberty of putting you with the First Division under General Joe Hooker. He has one of the best mess arrangements in the army."

"Thank you for your attention, Major. It's much appreciated. What is your name?"

"Cochran, sir. James Cochran. I'm in charge of the General's Headquarter Provost Guard. The Sergeant here will take you to your billet and then show you the road to the gun park. If I can be of any further assistance, please ask."

"Thank you very much, Major. I think you've answered all my needs and given me good advice which I shall take."

Cochran saluted. Arthur replied, and then followed the Sergeant to his new billet.

Having stashed his kit, and managed to get some bread and cold beef from the Staff Mess, Arthur rode out of town on the Gaithersburg road towards the artillery positions, which, when he reached them, he could see had the guns and limbers laid out in a similar way to a British battery. As he rode by, a number of the Union gunners watched him, and they were obviously mystified by his uniform.

At one group of guns he spotted an officer who was also looking back at him. Arthur reined in, dismounted and leading his horse, he walked over to the man who he could see by the two double bars on his shoulder boards was a Captain.

"Good afternoon, Captain. I am Colonel Rutland of the British Royal Artillery on attachment to General McClellan's Army."

The Captain snapped a smart salute. "Good afternoon, sir. How can I help?"

"As I'm here to report to the British Government on the Union use of artillery, I'd like to be shown around

Rutland's Blues and Greys

your Battery if that is possible. I have here a letter of introduction from the General's HQ as proof of my identity." He handed over his letter of authority.

The Captain read it and said, "Thank you sir, that all looks in order." He called to a private standing by a gun. "Jamieson, take the Colonel's horse to the lines."

Facing Arthur he said. "My name is Captain John Reynolds, and this is L Battery of the 1st New York Regiment."

"Thank you, Captain. I'd like it if you would simply show me around your Battery and the pieces. If I have any questions, perhaps I can ask them as we go along."

"Certainly, sir."

Reynolds, who was of medium height and slimly built, had a finely chiselled face with deep set eyes. He wore a trimmed beard that it seemed most Union officers sported. He led Arthur towards the guns which were standing in a straight row. "We were formed from the Rochester, New York area in September '61 and mustered to the Union Army in October," he explained.

Arthur looked at the line of guns and saw one had badly damaged wheels to the limber and gun carriage.

Reynolds saw him looking at it and said, "That happened a few days ago when we had a run in with the Rebs at Bull Run."

Arthur nodded. "Have you got all other repairs done?" he asked.

"Oh sure, Colonel, we've sorted out one hell of a lot of trouble. Now we just need a few wheels and more ammunition and my boys are ready to go all over again."

"Was it bad?" asked Arthur.

Reynolds looked at him, then he looked at the medals on Arthur's chest. "I take it you have seen action, Colonel."

"Yes," replied Arthur nodding his head, "and I have always found it bad. Even when we've won, there are the dead of our enemies around us and often some of our comrades. It's always bad."

"We didn't lose many men but we sure had to move around a lot to stop being surrounded." Reynolds looked back at the guns. "The boys worked damned hard but they came out well." There was a pause. Arthur did not interrupt.

"But we're ready to give them a thrashing next time, that's for sure," murmured Reynolds.

"How many of your men are regular army?"

"None, Colonel. We're all Americans first, and Army second. I raised this Battery from my hometown area. It wasn't difficult. I said I was for the Union and going to defend it – and the rest of them thought the same way."

Arthur was amazed. "That's incredible. You raised this Battery yourself by working on the patriotism of men in your town?"

Reynolds smiled. "That's right, Colonel."

"But having raised the Battery, you actually had to learn gunnery skills from scratch just like the others? I've never heard of anything like that before."

Reynolds laughed. "Well, Colonel, you'll hear it a lot more like that when you ask around."

Rutland's Blues and Greys

"Captain, I admire your dedication and tenacity." Arthur walked over to the guns, which were parked in line.

"I understand that you're in the First Army Corps under General Hooker. Is that right?" asked Arthur.

"Yes, sir. We are in its First Division. Our commander is Brigadier Doubleday."

"How many Infantry Regiments are in the Division?"

"I think there are about 16 or 17 in four separate Brigades."

"And how many Batteries are there in the Corps?"

"Four."

"Four!" exclaimed Arthur. "You mean just four batteries of six guns for 16 regiments!"

"Yes, they are 1st Battery New Hampshire, Battery D 1st Rhode Island, Battery B 4th United States and us. You sound surprised, Colonel."

"I'm astounded. In Europe we'd have three or four times that amount of artillery for a division of this size."

Reynolds took off his cap, scratched his head, and then replaced his cap. "I think I'm right in saying that this division has more artillery than any of the divisions in the army."

"That is amazing."

"What do you use all that artillery for, Colonel?" asked the Captain.

Arthur faced him wondering if he was joking or being facetious but Reynolds was obviously absolutely serious. It was then that Arthur realised that these volunteer officers were not trained in the use of artillery, just in how to serve it. So he started to explain what to him was an incredibly obvious fact, in basic gunnery terms.

"Firstly, the guns are used to destroy the opposing artillery. Then when our army commander knows where the enemy infantry is, he will instruct the guns to pound their positions until they have been reduced and our infantry can attack."

"Do the guns advance with the infantry?" asked Reynolds.

"Hopefully they can be positioned to continue firing on the enemy position right up until the infantry are close enough to charge. They will be angle enfilading fire from the side, or fire over the heads of the advancing infantry."

"How about in defence?"

"The guns should be set far enough back so that they can create a killing ground in front of the infantry's defensive position. They can pound the advancing enemy right up to the time they charge."

Reynolds was frowning. "Do your guns fire at close ranges of say two hundred yards?" he asked.

"Very rarely," said Arthur, "as by that time they are vulnerable to the attacking infantry, and their own infantry are in retreat. Then the guns would use canister or grape. But this is very rare."

"I think you are in for a surprise, Colonel," said Reynolds with a smile.

The two men continued their walk around the gun park, with Arthur asking questions which were often answered with statements that surprised him further.

After an hour of walking, and talking with Reynolds, Arthur arrived at the tented battery office.

"Captain, I received some advice which I think is sound," said Arthur. "I was told to attach myself to a specific group of gunners so I can see and get to know a battery and how it works in action. I'm going to ride out to see more Union Artillery but if I may, can I attach myself to your Battery ? I think I've a great deal to learn from you all."

Reynolds smiled "We'll be pleased to have you travel with us, sir, but I think we might learn from you more than we can teach you. Have you had a long and varied career with your artillery?"

Arthur nodded. "Yes. In the last twenty odd years I've fought with the guns in Afghanistan, the Crimea, and India. I've seen a great deal of the Asian world - but here in the United States, this is all very different. To be very honest, Captain, being a military observer is completely new to me. Somehow I'm uneasy about watching a battle without taking part." Arthur looked around the gun park. "It is all very unnatural for me," he said half to himself.

He turned back to Reynolds. "But don't think, Captain, I'll interfere with you in any way when you're in action. I'll be to one side and you can completely forget about me. Personally I'd hate to have a senior officer close by when I have Battery responsibilities in a battle."

Reynolds gestured to a Gunner to bring up Arthur's horse. Then he said. "Colonel, do please visit us whenever you wish. Tomorrow we are doing some practice drilling to finish training the replacements for the men we lost at the last Bull Run battle."

"Thank you, Captain. I shall take up that offer."

Arthur mounted his horse and continued his ride through the enormous camp of the assembled Army of the Potomac. As he rode through the chosen military position, he saw the usual paraphernalia of an army encampment. Though he had seen this scene in a number of countries, from India to Russia, it always intrigued and amazed him, yet surprisingly, this Army was somehow different. There were the usual lines of tents but now there were the large conical Sibley tents which held 20 men, plus the 'A' tents for individual officers or six men. This was the basic static living area but around this were the all-enveloping movements, sounds and smells of an army. The smoke from numerous cooking fires rose into the air to be mixed with the aromas, good and bad, of the regimental or company cooking. Then there was the wholesome smell of the horses in their lines as a complement to the rest of the aromas.

He could see squads of men practising for war. Men who had been tradesmen or labourers a few months before were now being shown the art of fighting and killing, with bayonets or rifle fire. The new soldiers, in their clean, dark-blue uniforms and their sturdy boots showed that they had never been against an enemy, or been in circumstances where they had had to scramble to save their own lives or to charge over a defeated enemy. These were the amateurs, an army being trained for a battle which would be their first - and for a number it would be their last – and it would be in a few days' or weeks' time.

Rutland's Blues and Greys

The shouts of the drill sergeants at squads of men to form line or change face or charge, all added to the mixture of the cacophony of sounds in the army encampment.

As he rode along the central road, one of the most striking things he saw was the number of flags, Union flags, Regimental flags, Battery flags and Cavalry guidons, all denoting the position of each minute part of this enormous army. Then he saw the main Headquarters area surrounded by pickets and guards - the high and mighty General Staff who were well protected from even the smallest threat.

Eventually he rode past the lines of canvas-topped supply wagons which would be used to take all the necessary food and equipment to support this massive field of men. Able to see down the long lines of carts, he counted them as he rode. He could see roughly how many wagons there were in each row and so by simple arithmetic he came to an astounding figure of over seven hundred wagons! The figures were incredible – just to think of the number of horses needed and the hay required for all of them.

Chapter 4

General Lee retired north, moving swiftly with the remaining part of his army. He quickly organised a defensive action behind him at South Mountain where he could delay McClellan as the large Federal army also tried to move north through the three main passes. This sharp action gave Lee just enough time to move his depleted army into a defensive position in the small town of Sharpsburg, which had a small river running on its east side called Antietam Creek. He had to hold the Federal Army back until 'Stonewall' Jackson could return from Harper's Ferry, which he had successfully taken with all its supplies.

Federal General McClellan, following close behind the Southern Army, gathered his 87,000 men on the east bank of Antietam Creek on September 16th 1862 so that he was ready for the battle that he would fight next day.

Late in the afternoon of the 16th September 1862, Arthur rode steadily along with the Army of the Potomac. He was attached to General Hooker's First

Rutland's Blues and Greys

Army Corps because L Battery was part of the artillery in the First Division.

As he rode the long and dusty road, he became aware that it was bordered with scenes that amazed and even shocked him by their normality. This was good quality farming country; the soil was rich and would give good yields. Here were families growing their crops of corn and tending their animals, and they were all about to be shattered by the horrors of war. None of these country folk had any experience of what was about to happen around them. Even Arthur had become aware that with the numbers and quality of the Union Army, they were a formidable force who were about to do battle with an equally strong force - both sides with modern weapons. The coming battle was going to be larger than anything Arthur had ever witnessed or been a part of. He felt very worried. He knew that his anguish was not downright fear - he had known that many times- but it was the worry of what this conflict would become in that it would almost certainly result in very large numbers of dead and wounded. Previously he had seen large battles in the Crimea but through the terrible chaos of that catastrophic war, both sides were basically static. Here the armies were moving and manoeuvring, so support was of the greatest importance.

As he rode, he started to hear from a distance the thump of the large guns being fired, and then he could see gun smoke rising from the low hills to his right - it had to be Union artillery firing into the Confederate lines at Sharpsburg. As he got closer to the town, he recognised the sound of the 20 pounders as they threw their shells out many hundreds of yards away. Eventually, as he got closer he could hear the bangs of the shells exploding.

Then from the distance came the popping of distant rifle fire. 'So the battle has started' he thought.

A Provost sergeant directed him towards General McClellan's Headquarters at Pry Farm - a farmhouse to the east of Sharpsburg set on raised ground a few hundred yards from the east bank of Antietam Creek.

Arthur reined in his horse close to a line of tents that had been set up behind the farmhouse. Slowly he slid out of the saddle, feeling stiff and weary. His legs and his backside were sore from the long and continuous riding, and he longed for a meal and a rest – then he had a large dose of self-criticism. In previous times when he had been in action with the British Army, he had been kept going by the excitement and tension, and with the knowledge that men depended on his decisions and action. Here he was just an observer, no one asked him for instructions or even an opinion. He was just watching – and hopefully keeping out of danger. He tied the reins to a hitching rope and walked towards the General's HQ.

An officer ran out of the farmhouse on a mission. Arthur recognised him as one of General McClellan's staff.

"Is there to be action, Major?" he asked.

"Yes, sir. The General is ready to attack early tomorrow morning."

"Thank you, Major," said Arthur and walked into the farmhouse. He wanted to find out the details of the planned battle and hopefully obtain a map of the area.

Two of the General's staff were standing by a table on which was spread a large campaign map. Arthur stood beside them and looked at it. He immediately understood what he saw. A line running almost north and south denoted a small winding river called the Antietam. To the west of it was the small town of Sharpsburg. Markers on the map to the north of the town denoted the suspected positions of the Southern forces. Arrows further north showed where the Federal forces were expected to attack and advance the next day. He could see artillery positions marked further north and east of the army, and it was there that he would now ride and stay during the battle. He also noticed arrows showing that, though the main attack would be from the north and north-east down the road from town called Hagerstown, there was also a force expecting to attack slightly below the town from the east. They were to cross the bridge over the stream and hit the right wing of Lee's army. Arthur pointed at the most northerly force.

"Who is that?" he asked.

"General Hooker's First Army Corps," was the reply. "With General Sumner supporting from his left."

Arthur pointed to the lower attack force who were to cross the bridge, "And who is that?" he asked.

"The Ninth Army Corps under Major General Burnside."

"When are they expected to start?"

"The same time as General Hooker. It is to be a two-front attack with the main blow from the north but Lee will have to take troops away from that front to defend against Burnside's attack."

Arthur nodded. It all seemed very sound. With General McClellan's overwhelming forces it was essential to attack Lee over as wide an area as possible, otherwise the Southerners could move their forces to defend each individual Union attack. It was obviously essential that McClellan's army had to all attack at the same time.

"I want to ride round to L Battery up to the north. Do you have a map of the town and its surrounds?" asked Arthur.

A clerk seated at a desk in the corner of the room said, "This is a local map without any positional markings on it, sir. Will that do?"

"That'll be fine," replied Arthur.

Arthur rode back to the track and headed up towards the north bridge to cross the Antietam Creek. Having crossed it he had to ride about three miles to swing round above the Union forces until he saw some artillery set on a slope that he could see from his map was close to the M. Miller Farm, presumably overlooking the battlefield, He rode over to them and saw that one of the batteries was L Battery with Captain Reynolds and his officers organising the ready position of the gun site.

Arthur took out his binoculars and examined the ground in front of the guns. It looked as though they would be firing over some woodland and onto a large cultivated area some 800 yards away. He did not approach Reynolds and had just decided to ride on to Hooker's Headquarters when the Captain strode over, saluted and said, "Well, sir, we're as ready as we ever will be." Arthur dismounted and, holding his horse's reins, stood beside the Battery Commander.

"May I ask your orders, Captain?"

"We are to be prepared to cover the large cornfield down there. The Rebs are supposed to be in those woods over to the west, well beyond the field. Either we will attack tomorrow or they will. Whichever, we are to be prepared for attack or defence."

Arthur nodded. He was rather surprised at the vagueness of the instructions. "I'm going to report to General Hooker's staff and I hope to observe the battle either with them or return here," he said as he put his foot into the stirrup and was about to mount when he added, "Remember, Captain, if you see me about tomorrow, please completely ignore me." He smiled at Reynolds. "And good luck."

He swung up into the saddle and returned Reynolds' salute. "I'll certainly come back to chat with you after the conflict when you have had a chance to rest."

"You'll be very welcome, sir."

Arthur turned his horse and followed the muddy tracks of the Union infantry, which swung north to cross the Smoketown Road until he saw a large farmhouse which, according to his map, had to be General Hooker's HQ at the J. Poffenberger Farm.

As he approached the farmhouse, he was stopped by a Provost Guard who, having asked him what he wanted, allowed Arthur to proceed. He rode round to the back of the farm and saw some horses on lines. He rode over and dismounted. A sergeant, who was wearing the leather apron of a farrier, took hold of the bridle. "We'll take care of your horse, sir."

"Thank you," replied Arthur. He pulled off his saddlebags and looked around for somewhere to stack them and make a sleeping place. The sergeant pointed to a large A tent. "I think you should report there, sir."

Arthur took the advice and was duly allocated a small A tent into which he put his saddlebags.

He awoke very early to the ripple of rifle fire and the thump of cannons. Dawn was only just breaking as he quickly pulled on his boots and jacket. He patted the sides of his field jacket and felt the slight bulkiness of the Millie pockets he had on either side. In each pocket, sewn on the inside of his jacket, were two very carefully folded bandages and a pad. Whenever he went on active service, Millie always insisted that he had them in his battledress. "Just in case you are wounded. At least you will have a clean bandage." He smiled at the recollection of her concern.

He picked up his saddlebags and went out to collect his horse, which was already saddled. From the wet ground he could see that there had been heavy rain during the night but he had slept soundly through it all. He found a line behind the farmhouse to hitch his horse to, and walked round to the front. The front yard of the farmhouse had numerous Union Staff Officers using their binoculars to look at the incredible scene in front of them. This position was perfect to view the right wing of the battlefield.

Arthur looked in the same direction as the other officers and saw a virtual amphitheatre. The ground in front of the farmhouse sloped gently down to a deep swathe of woods running left to right. Looking over the woods he could see that beyond them was a large cultivated area, part of which was a crop of maize that stood some four to five foot tall. To his left were the woods that L Battery would be firing over.

About 1000 yards to his right front were more woods and set behind them and up a gentle hill he could see Confederate guns firing. He looked at his map and saw that these guns were on Nicodemus Heights.

Beyond the cornfield, the ground sloped gently upwards from the right and the Hagerstown Pike, directly in front of which was an orchard and, according to his map, the Miller farmhouse - both almost beside the road.

Arthur pulled his binoculars out and, in the early morning light, focused them on the field. In the tall crop of maize he could see that a terrible battle was being fought. He could see lines of men in blue pouring from the woods to his left. They were running forward and then being swept away by devastating rifle and artillery fire. As he watched the Union attack crumble, he saw opposing infantry in Grey rise and move through this ruination of a crop, charging back at the Union infantry. Obviously these men had been hidden in the cornfield and now, completely exposed, were fighting a terrible conflict.

Arthur raised his glasses to see the devastating Confederate gunfire that was coming from the Nicodemus Heights. But there, almost a mile away to his right front, he could see what looked like a small church. He orientated his map and saw that it was the Dunker Church. Focussing his glasses on it, he watched, as close to it, more Confederate artillery started to pour accurate fire onto the cornfield in excellent support of their infantry when the Union soldiers attacked.

He scanned down the right of the battlefield close to the farm and orchard near the road, and stopped!

There to his amazement a battery of Union guns was coming in to action. This was madness! Why were they so close? They were so vulnerable to the rifle fire from the Greys who were only 200 odd yards away. In fact it was just a half battery. As they came in to action, he could see that they were the bronze Napoleon guns, ideal for short range use - but not such close quarters. Despite the gunners falling as they were being hit, they managed to fire one round each at the Confederate infantry and, after the smoke lifted, Arthur expected to see the advancing Greys torn apart, but they did not seem to be hurt at all. Again the three guns fired - but with little effect while their gunners were being hit badly by the bullets of the Southern infantry. Then Arthur realised what was happening - they were firing too high! He wanted to shout out their error. The elevating screws were set too high and the shot and canister were flying harmlessly over the rebel infantry. As he watched in agony at the gunners dropping, he saw the tall figure of a senior Union officer mounted on a dark horse gallop up, throw himself off his horse and run down to the guns. Waving his arms and shouting he told the gunners what they were doing wrong, and, after a short pause, the next shots of canister from the Napoleons tore away the fencing directly in front of them and wiped out whole groups of the massed infantry. This senior Union officer then remained with the guns and continued to help serve the guns because of the lack of gunners to feed the ever-hungry barrels. Without him they would have been lost to a man - but these guns, set ridiculously too close to the enemy, actually held the wave of attackers back.

Arthur scanned back and towards the woods to his left just further up the slope. More Union infantry were debouching from them to stream onto the bloody field - but again they were stopped and then thrown back by devastating gunfire. L Battery must be one of the batteries who were supporting these attacks, he thought.

He lowered his binoculars, slid them back into their case, and then, looking down at his hands, realised that they were shaking as the pent-up emotion of seeing the horrors on this terrible battlefield hit him. In his career he had seen mass death before, seen incredible slaughter, lost comrades at his shoulder, but he had been there in the fighting but as a participant, not a bystander, a cold observer.

To be a close witness to this scene knowing that these incredible actions were not fired by blind obedience nor by alcohol or drugs, nor by religious fanaticism, was incredible. This mass heroism was induced by simple belief in their way of life, their own nationalism, loyalty to their state – it was almost unbelievable, except he had seen it.

Slowly, his head bowed in thought, he walked back through to the farmhouse, through the front door and into the main front room where two staff officers were standing by a table, examining a large battlefield map.

Arthur saluted. "Good morning, gentlemen. Can you assist me, please?"

The two officers, one of whom was a Colonel, looked up at Arthur and the Colonel said. "And who are you, sir?"

"I beg your pardon, Colonel. I am Colonel Rutland, Royal Artillery, attached to General McClellan's staff as an observer," explained Arthur. "I've been watching the battle's progress out on the cornfield, but I understand that this is the Federal right wing. Can you please show me how to reach the left wing?"

"Certainly, Colonel," replied the Federal Colonel and turned the battle map to show Arthur. "We are here at the Poffenberger farmhouse. General Hooker is attacking south towards Sharpsburg town. General Sumner is somewhere to our left but we are not sure exactly where, or how we are supporting them or they us." He pointed to the left-hand part of the map that showed a bridge over the small Antietam River. "General Burnside, who is our left flank, is attacking the rebel right over the bridge."

"Over the bridge?" queried Arthur. A whole division attacking the enemy flank by crossing over just one bridge – it seemed impossible.

"Yes, sir. He is doing so as we speak."

Arthur took out his map and showed it to the Colonel, who said. "Cross the Smoketown Road and ride cross-country up to the North Bridge. Then follow the river bank south. Take care, as we are not sure where the Rebs are exactly nor where you will be safe from their fire."

Arthur folded up his map, put it back into his pocket, then saluted and said, "Thank you, gentlemen, for your assistance."

Rutland's Blues and Greys

He left General Hooker's HQ, unhitched his horse, mounted it and started back up the Hagerstown Pike. He had a four to five mile ride round the whole Federal army which he thought would take him a couple of hours or so. He looked at his fob watch – amazingly it was only 9am. All that death in just a few hours.

Firstly, Arthur retraced his tracks of the day before and rode east towards the position that had been held by L Battery. He found that they had been moved quite a lot closer to the battle in the cornfield.

He dismounted and keeping well to the rear he could see that the battery was heavily engaged with the whole gun site regularly covered in gun smoke. The shells were being fired at the far side of the cornfield in support of the Union Infantry. Occasionally a round shot or shell flew inwards from the Confederate artillery but it was only sporadic and totally ignored by the Union gunners. The sleek three-inch rifled cannon were being used very hard and firing at an impressively steady rate. The barrels must have been heating up but the gunners were still keeping up the support for the infantry. He moved well over to the side of the battery and watched as each gun fired. It was quite easy to follow each shell and spot where it was landing, and he was very surprised to see that the grouping of the shot was amazingly tight and accurate.

Through the familiar bangs of the guns firing he suddenly heard the whirr of a rifle bullet as it flew close to him. He looked over to his left front, then pulled out his binoculars and focused them on the rise of a slope some 300 yards away and there saw that a number of Southern sharpshooters had managed to get that close to the battery without being seen. A Battery horse screamed and fell down, hit by a Confederate bullet. The whole of L Battery was busy on their fire instructions and were unaware of this terrible close danger. A second bullet flew very close to Arthur, so close that he crouched down in the saddle in reflex, but no one at the Battery had noticed this dangerous threat. He kicked his spurs into his horse and galloped the short distance to where he could see Captain Reynolds standing behind the guns.

"Captain!" he shouted. Reynolds turned round, and Arthur pulled in his horse to skid to a stop close to the Battery Commander who caught hold of the horse's bridle.

Arthur pointed with his left arm out to the side and called down. "Sharpshooters are close to your left. They are firing at you now."

Reynolds released the bridle and, calling one of his Lieutenants, ran through the gun smoke to the left section guns. Two gunners were hit and the Sergeant of the left gun had just seen the Confederate riflemen.

"Swing your gun round!" shouted Reynolds waving his arm towards the danger. "Use canister."

"It's loaded with shell, sir."

"Fire it at them, then use canister."

The Sergeant and his gun crew threw themselves onto the cannon and swung it round. He wound up the elevation screw to depress the muzzle and called the order 'Fire".

The shot slammed into the soil in front of the sharpshooters' line but did not explode. It was too close-range.

Rutland's Blues and Greys

The gunners loaded the gun with canister so that the tin case of heavy iron balls would spread out shotgun fashion and wipe out anyone it fired at. The Confederate riflemen were still firing and another gunner fell down holding his leg.

The Gun Sergeant, having adjusted the elevation screw a little lower, waited until the piece was loaded, then shouted, "Fire!"

This time the result was much more dramatic. They had aimed low and the fire was deadly. The case tore into the soil and air around the Confederates - the rest of them crouched lower and drew back from the edge of the slope.

"Keep hitting them until you think they are gone," ordered Reynolds. "Keep an eye on them in case they return."

"Yes, sir," replied the Sergeant.

Arthur had slowly ridden away some fifty yards behind the battery and watched the action. As Reynolds turned to go back to his command post, he looked up, saw Arthur standing behind the guns and waved. Arthur acknowledged with a raised arm and turned his horse to retire further behind the battery.

Chapter 5

He watched the battery for another fifteen minutes, then walked his horse away and rode along a number of narrow farm tracks dropping down towards the Antietam Creek. Eventually he saw a group of Union infantry who were guarding a stone bridge across the creek. High to his right front he could see Pry House, General McClellan's HQ. Using his map he could see that it was about two miles from Sharpsburg and the main fighting, and he wondered how much could be seen from that position by the senior staff.

It was a stiff ride up to the farmhouse, in front of which, on an open area, were a number of people who seemed to be a mixture of Army personnel and civilians. Arthur rode up to the farmhouse, dismounted, hitched his horse to the rail, and then walked towards the large group.

On the front edge of the people looking towards the battle field were a group of Union officers. Amongst them Arthur recognised the small figure of General McClellan; he was talking animatedly to his officers

Rutland's Blues and Greys

and occasionally looking through his field glasses towards the smoke covered battlefield.

Arthur walked closer to the rest of the large group and looked around and listened. They seemed to be mainly civilians, some making notes, others talking, laughing and drinking coffee and whisky. Possibly they were from newspapers or some similar connection. He noticed that there were a few foreign observers similar to himself there - these were obviously taking the safe approach to witnessing the battle. For a few minutes he watched McClellan as he strutted back and forth, and could hear the General speaking in loud tones but it was not clear enough for Arthur to understand the content. McClellan seemed to be enjoying the situation and absorbing the hero worship given to him as 'Little Mac'.

Arthur, unimpressed by the scene, walked back into the house hoping to find a good source of information.

He passed a large room which he could see had two tables laid out with masses of food, presumably for lunch. Suddenly Arthur felt his hunger pangs as he realised had had no breakfast and now he was ravenous. He picked up two rolls, still warm from the baking, and tore then open. Into them he put slices of ham and some cheese. He had just finished filling them when a smartly dressed Lieutenant, wearing white gloves, walked smartly up to him and said, "Excuse me, sir!"

Arthur smiled at the catering officer and said, "Thank you, I haven't had any breakfast yet."

"But.." exclaimed the Lieutenant.

Arthur waved his free hand and as he walked to the door, he said, "Don't worry, Lieutenant, I shall be back for the lunch." With the two well-filled rolls in his hands Arthur walked out of the house, over to his horse and, with some difficulty, mounted it. Slowly, eating his rolls, he rode round behind Pry House and followed the lane away to the east - after a short time it joined the road which he saw from his map was the Boonsboro Pike.

In half a mile he came across a regiment of infantry who were spread out along the road. The men were sitting or lying down beside the track on the grass, while a few officers and senior NCOs stood close to the road edge. As he approached, a tall, well-built officer sporting a large drooping moustache with ends below his chin line, walked towards Arthur as though wanting to speak to him.

"Do you have any orders for us?" asked the officer, who Arthur could see by his shoulder boards was a Lieutenant Colonel.

"I'm afraid not, Colonel. I'm an observer from the British Army so I cannot assist."

"Oh right, sir. My regiment has been told to be ready to move."

"Are you in General Burnside's Army Corps?"

"No, sir. We are the 20th Maine in General Porter's Fifth Army Corps. I am Lieutenant Colonel Chamberlain."

Arthur slid off his horse and offered his hand. "Pleased to meet you, Colonel. I am Colonel Rutland."

Chamberlain took his hand and said, "Are you a professional British soldier, Colonel?"

"Yes," replied Arthur. "But this is my first battle acting as an observer, and I find it very strange."

Rutland's Blues and Greys

"And this is my first battle," said Chamberlain. "So it is an anxious moment for me."

"Have no fear, Colonel," said Arthur. "Your training will carry you through."

"Training sir? A month or so ago I was a lecturer at Bowdoin College. I have been a Lieutenant Colonel for just five weeks!"

Arthur's face showed amazement. "But what did you lecture on?"

"Debate and rhetoric."

"My goodness!" exclaimed Arthur. "Are your men experienced?"

"I have a Major and two Sergeants who are regulars, while the rest of us are volunteers of a few weeks' standing."

Arthur was silent – speechless. Inside his head he thought 'How can you send a regiment of untrained men led by inexperienced officers to fight against an enemy armed with modern weapons like this?'

"You are nonplussed, Colonel?" asked Chamberlain.

"Exactly," replied Arthur. "I can offer no comment other than to say that I trust you do not see any action today."

"But Colonel, we're all eager to fight."

"I hope you have a few more months' training before your eagerness is satisfied," said Arthur. "Now can you please point me towards the lower bridge, where I understand General Burnside is making an attack?"

Chamberlain pointed down the road to his left. "I think the bridge is somewhere close around that bend."

"Many thanks, Colonel. I hope we meet again." He saluted and mounted his horse.

Chamberlain returned the salute. "I look forward to it, sir."

Arthur smiled, then turned his horse's head down the road and spurred the animal to a canter.

As he rode, he could hear the large Union guns firing at targets near the town but as he went further south the sound of gunfire slowly receded until he could just hear rifle fire ahead of him. He was going towards an attack point of a whole Army Corps! Why was there no supporting gunfire?

Eventually he was forced to take a track up to his left as the slopes beside the creek became steep and high. Reaching the top he cantered his horse for about a mile until he could hear the rattle of rifle fire again. He crested a small hill and below him was the amazing scene of the Federal attack as they tried to use one narrow, stone bridge to cross over Antietam Creek which was barely 50 feet wide. The other side of the creek was dominated by a high wooded bluff, which had numerous large boulders strewn on it. The Greys were using these, and shallow trenches, to protect themselves and dominate the whole Union attack area. A continuous rippling cloud of powder smoke showed where a large number of Confederate troops were firing, in comparative safety, into the massed Union regiment below.

The Blue attackers were streaming alongside the creek edge towards the stone bridge which appeared to be only 12 feet wide. He looked at his map and saw that it was called the Rohrbach Bridge. As they streamed towards the crossing, the massed infantry were a perfect and easy target for the Rebels firing from the hill. The Greys were firing as fast as they could load - and most of their bullets hit a target that would have been hard to miss. All this was before the Union regiment even started to cross the bridge.

Arthur pulled out his field glasses and scanned his side of the bank to see where the Union guns were situated. There were none there! He could not understand it - this was the perfect situation for artillery to clear the entrenched enemy from the front - but there were no guns there!

He pushed his horse on to slowly descend the slope towards the creek. Some 400 yards short he found a cluster of trees where he tethered his horse in comparative safety and went forward in a crouch to peer from the trees onto the battle scene.

Above him to his left he could see a knot of officers, presumably General Burnside's staff, who were in a perfect position to see what was happening. Yet down there was a regiment trying on its own to cross this small bridge completely unsupported by artillery - or even other rifle fire.

When the remaining infantrymen reached the bridge, they bunched up and charged but the Greys massed rifle fire into the Union front and sides slammed them back with ease. The front ranks of the attackers simply dropped onto the road of the stone bridge and became the main impediment that their own comrades had to struggle over to get past. It was appalling.

He sat down and stayed watching the ridiculous and terrible wasteful use of men for over an hour as one regiment after another tried doing exactly the same as the previous attack. He studiously sketched the scene into his gunner's notebook so that he could refer to it when he was writing up his report. It would confirm to him the horrendous facts that were happening in front of his eyes.

There was no sign of any Federal artillery but shells, from Confederate guns situated high up close to the town, landed occasionally into the seething mass of Union soldiers.

Eventually at about midday a Union regiment charged from a different line directly down the hill and straight towards the bridge. They attacked with such force and determination that they managed to cross the bridge, possibly because the Confederates were low or even out of ammunition. Other infantry regiments then followed and Arthur watched as the Greys gradually relinquished their trenches and cover.

He untethered his horse and rode it down towards the creek where the evidence of this terrible and unnecessary loss of life was, in its full horror, spread all around. Here was the product of an obscenely useless General.

As he slowly rode alongside the creek, his mind filled with the scenes of this gross incompetence, he was shaken out of his deep contemplation by a voice shouting at him.

"Who are you, sir?"

Arthur looked up and saw a staff Major, who had ridden up beside him.

Rutland's Blues and Greys

"Colonel Rutland, military observer accredited to General McClellan and with General Hooker."

"General Burnside thought so and has instructed me to tell you that while you are in his area of attack, you are to remain back with the other observers away from the action."

Wearily Arthur nodded. "Very well," he said. "Please convey my apologies to the General for any inconvenience I have caused."

The Major saluted and turned his horse to canter back to the General's staff. Arthur also turned his horse away from this bloody bridge and started the long ride back towards L Battery and General Hooker's left wing.

He rode slowly following the same tracks he had used before, resting his horse and allowing it to drink from the creek at the bridge he had crossed earlier. There was probably a quicker route but he needed time to think about all that he had seen in this horrendous day. Eventually he reached L Battery position and rode past. He did not stop, knowing that he would not be a very popular guest just after a battle. So he continued his slow and weary way back towards General Hooker's HQ.

He was just approaching the Poffenberger Farm when he saw an officer cantering towards him. It was a staff Captain who pulled his horse to a sudden sliding halt as he came abreast of Arthur.

"Colonel Rutland?" he asked.

"Yes."

"General Hooker would like to see you at once, sir. Will you please follow me?" Arthur was about to query this instruction but the officer turned his horse on the spot and from a standing start, cantered off towards Hooker's Headquarters.

Arthur spurred his weary horse to catch up with the swiftly moving Captain, then decided that he was only going to trot after him until they reached the HQ.

"This way, Colonel," called the Captain. Arthur was amazed at the urgency of the instruction and the instant action that was taking place. He followed the officer towards the front entrance of the farmhouse.

Both men entered the main hall and stopped outside a closed double door.

"Wait here please, sir," said the Captain. Arthur could hear raised voices coming from inside. One man was obviously laying down the law to someone else.

"Will you go in now, Colonel?" Arthur walked through the door and into a large dining room where General Hooker was seated at a table, his leg propped up on the seat of a chair. The leg was bandaged below the knee where he had received a wound during the morning's fighting. Three other officers, who Arthur could see were all Colonels, were standing in front of him. They had apparently been the butt of Hooker's anger. Arthur saluted and stood to attention in front of the table.

"And here is more trouble for me," said Hooker loudly. "Colonel, you are a bloody nuisance to me and my staff."

Arthur was astounded at the outburst and annoyed that it was happening in front of other officers. Before he could ask why he was such a 'bloody nuisance', Hooker continued. "General Burnside has said you are a bloody nuisance and General McClellan has himself ordered me to stop you being a bloody nuisance."

Hooker leaned forward resting his arms on the tabletop. "You're wondering why you are such a bloody nuisance to all these senior generals. Well, the answer is simple. You're getting too close to the action. If you get killed, none of us give a damn. If you get wounded, well, that keeps you out of trouble, but what if you get captured? Wow, we're all in trouble then. You are a representative of the Government who we hope will soon show support for us."

Hooker looked intently at Arthur. "Colonel, for goodness sake, why don't you do what all the other military observers do, observe from the safety of General McClellan's or my Headquarters? Do that and we would all be happy. Will you do that for me?"

As this tirade was descending on Arthur, he felt that, under all the so-called fury, there was a element of understanding from the General.

"I do apologise to all the Generals and their staff for the inconvenience I have caused them," said Arthur. "But I regret that I must feel free to go wherever I want – and I want to see, close up, how the Union artillery works. Views from Headquarters are often indistinct."

Hooker smiled. "Damn you, Colonel. All I want is a quiet life to whip the rebels, and you come along and make my life uncomfortable." He paused. "Hell, Colonel, if I was in your place, I'd do exactly what you're doing, and if you were in my place, you'd do what I am doing. I'm getting a kicking from higher up, so I'm kicking you."

"Thank you, sir. I consider myself kicked."

"You don't get off that easily, Colonel." Hooker wagged his finger at Arthur. "I have been instructed to provide someone to assist you."

Arthur frowned. " I will not be controlled, sir."

"I'll bet you won't, so I'm getting a sergeant to accompany you and assist you with everything you need for your safety and comfort."

Arthur gave a slight smile. A sergeant as an advisor and carer! He would not have any worth except as a token.

"Now Colonel, this sergeant will have incredible powers. He can arrest you, imprison you and even have you shot if necessary, so please behave yourself as General McClellan would like you to."

Arthur could hardly stop himself from laughing out loud. General Hooker had complied with his senior's instruction but with a sergeant! An NCO could have no control over a Colonel, especially one of a foreign power.

"Thank you, sir, for your care and attention. I'll do all that I can not to cause any further trouble."

"Thank you, Colonel."

Arthur drew himself to attention, saluted, and then turned to leave. As he did, he heard Hooker say to the other Colonels. "Hell, gentlemen, if you had as much enthusiasm as that, I'd be a happy man."

Chapter 6

That evening Arthur was seated in a canvas chair under the awning outside his tent while a small comforting fire burned close by.

"Colonel Rutland, sir?"

Arthur looked up to see a tall infantry Sergeant, with a tanned face framed by long dark brown hair, standing there. In fact on his sleeve the diamond shape above his three stripes showed he was a First Sergeant.

"Yes, Sergeant, you want me?"

"Yes, sir. I have been posted by order of General Hooker to be your assistant."

"My assistant!" exclaimed Arthur.

"Yes, sir."

Arthur felt in a mischievous mood. "Right, Sergeant, what are your specific duties?"

"Duties, sir?"

"Yes. Specific duties."

"Ah, well, sir."

"Sergeant, I'm sure that when you were posted to be my assistant, whoever ordered you to the position told you of your specific duties and responsibilities. Didn't they?"

"Ah, yes, sir."

"Well?"

"I was told to um, er. "

"Make sure I did not get in to mischief?"

"Oh no, sir." The Sergeant shuffled his feet. "Er, I was told that um, er."

Arthur could not taunt the poor man any further. It was not his fault that some superior had put him into an impossible situation.

"Sit down, Sergeant."

"Sit down, sir?"

"Yes, sit down. I want to talk to you."

"Very good, sir." The Sergeant sat on a stool close to the fire obviously feeling very awkward and ill at ease.

"What is your name, Sergeant?"

"Forrester, sir."

"And your Christian name?"

"Rafferty, sir."

"Well, Rafferty, you and I are going to get on very well. You don't believe it now but in a couple of days you'll agree with me."

Arthur offered Rafferty a cigar. "Do you smoke?"

"Well.."

"Take a cigar, Sergeant. Then we can have a civilised chat."

Forrester was obviously stunned by the way the conversation was going. "Well, thank you, sir."

Together Colonel and Sergeant drew on their cigars and blew the smoke into the early evening air.

Rutland's Blues and Greys

"So, Sergeant Forrester, you are stuck with this detail, looking after a blasted English officer who won't do as he's told."

Forrester coughed on the smoke. "Oh no, sir."

"Oh yes, sir," said Arthur with a laugh. "Now look, you and I have obviously got to agree on your position because someone on high has told you to look after me. Why? Because I want to see the fighting at close hand and your Generals don't want me to get captured."

Very wisely Forrester did not make any comment. "So, Sergeant, I'll be more careful in future, I promise, and I'll listen to your advice regarding my safety. But I am still going to go where I want to when I think it is truly essential. Now where will you be billeted?"

"Oh, I shall be at the General's Headquarters with the Provost section."

"What!" exclaimed Arthur. "You're a Provost Sergeant?"

"Yes, sir." Forrester shifted uncomfortably on his seat.

"Well, Sergeant," mused Arthur. "That means we must work even harder to get the right answer to this problem and it must be to my liking and to your orders."

Arthur stared into the embers of the fire, gently drawing on his cigar. "Who do you have to report to and how often?"

"I have to report to General Hooker's ADC when necessary."

"When necessary," repeated Arthur. "That means when I get into danger, ignoring your suggestions. Right?"

"Well.."

"Sergeant, we aren't going to get anywhere unless you are honest with me. Am I right?"

"Yes, sir."

"Now, do you think you could go to the ADC to say that we've had a chat and that I've agreed not to put myself unnecessarily in danger but that you must have a horse to be able to accompany me wherever I go?"

"Oh yes, sir."

"Good. I shall either be in my billet with the General's staff or I'll be at one of the batteries, in which case you needn't stay with me because I'll not leave the battery billet except in extreme circumstances. Will you tell him that?"

"Yes, sir."

"Right, now what I want in exchange for this soft life I'll be giving you is some of the good things found at the Staff billets. At times I'll want food and drink from the Staff Mess while I am with the batteries. Are you prepared to bring that to me?"

"Yes, sir."

"Excellent," said Arthur. "Rafferty, you can stay as close to me as you wish during the day, subject to the times when I wish to discuss points with a senior officer. Then I expect you to be in the background."

Arthur looked at Forrester. "If you are diplomatic, we should rub along very well."

The Sergeant smiled. "I think we will, sir."

"Now tell me, where do you come from?" asked Arthur.

"I was born in Brooklyn. I lived with my parents until I decided I wanted to leave and join the Army."

Rutland's Blues and Greys

"So you are a Regular soldier?"

"Yes, sir."

"Then you can have no fear, Sergeant. I won't intentionally let you down. Is your father army?"

"No sir, he's a policeman in New York."

"And your mother?"

"She is a milliner. She designs ladies hats for a small specialist firm."

"She sounds a very enterprising lady."

Forrester smiled and looked down "Oh yes, sir. She is a one-off."

"Meaning?"

"Her family feel that she married below herself."

Then Forrester told of how his mother came from a doctor's family in New Hampshire and how they felt she could have done better than marry a New York policeman. He continued his tale in some detail but then paused - and looked at Arthur, who he saw was deep in thought. The Colonel was gazing myopically into the fire. There was a total silence only broken by the occasional crackle from the burning logs. The sergeant fidgeted on his chair. He felt ill at ease with the situation - this officer who seemed so welcoming and friendly was now almost in a trance.

Arthur stirred from his deep contemplation, lifted his head and turned to face Forrester. "Sergeant, we have only just met but I'm about to make a confession to you." Forrester shifted on his stool with embarrassment and apprehension.

"While you were talking, it dawned on me what I've been doing." Arthur fell silent and again stared at the fire. Then he said in a quiet voice almost as though he was speaking just to himself, "For the first time in my career I have watched a terrible battle but been without responsibility or even in danger."

He drew on his cigar. "I now realise that I was so ill at ease with my position of viewing from complete safety that I felt I had to put myself in some sort of danger to try and be at one with all those men fighting out there." Again he paused. "General Hooker is right. I am a bloody nuisance."

Arthur lifted his head and looking at Forrester said, "No more, Sergeant. I going to do what I was sent out here to do, even if that means I stay back at HQ with the other observers."

He smiled and smacked his hand on his knee. "Well, that makes life a lot easier for both us, Sergeant. Go back to your billet now and come and find me here, or at L Battery, tomorrow morning. Then we will set off together."

Forrester stood up and saluted. "Very good, sir. I'll report to you tomorrow and I'll have a horse."

"Good night, Sergeant."

"Good night, sir"

Arthur looked back in to the flames from the camp fire. In the past few minutes he had sorted out a problem that an hour ago he did not know he even had.

Next morning as Arthur and Forrester rode around the Army encampment, they passed a line of tents belonging to an infantry regiment. Outside one of the Sibley tents, he saw the droop-moustached face of the Colonel who he had last seen yesterday alongside the Antietam Creek. It was indeed Lieutenant Colonel

Chamberlain seated at a table having a cup of coffee. He got up quickly and strode towards Arthur.

"Good morning, Colonel," he said. "Will you join me in a mug of coffee?"

"I would be delighted, Colonel, thank you."

Arthur dismounted and Chamberlain called out, "Kilrain, take the Colonel's horse, please."

A squat, scruffily dressed corporal replied in a rich Irish brogue, "Certainly, Colonel." He took the reins and led Arthur's horse away while Forrester followed.

The two Colonels walked over to the table outside the tent and Chamberlain said, "Please take a seat." An infantryman instantly appeared with a full mug of hot black coffee that he put on the table in front of Arthur.

"That will certainly wake me up," exclaimed Arthur.

"So, Colonel," said Chamberlain. "From a professional English Army officer's point of view, 'How went the day?'"

Arthur took a sip of his coffee, and slowly put the mug back onto the table. 'Here's a problem,' he thought. 'Tell the truth and destroy their confidence however weakly based it was – or tell a lie.'

Seeing Arthur's hesitation, Chamberlain said. "Will it help, Colonel, if I add the words 'in confidence'?"

Arthur smiled. "Firstly," he said, "I am Colonel Arthur Rutland of Her Majesty's Royal Artillery. Please call me Arthur."

Chamberlain nodded. "And I, Arthur, am Lieutenant Colonel Lawrence Chamberlain, Second in Command of the 20th Maine, until a few weeks ago Professor of Debate and Rhetoric at Bowdoin College."

Arthur looked across the field and the lines of regimental tents. " Lawrence," he asked. "How many of your men are married? How many have children?"

With a slight frown Lawrence replied, "I don't rightly know. Should I?"

Arthur shook his head. "No," he murmured. "That was not a rational question. But I cannot rationalise this type of fighting." He looked again at the long lines of tents and the general bustle of activity.

"My problem is this simple use of mass infantry as in the Crimea, but without any manoeuvre just because your men are untrained for anything except a steady frontal attack." He looked at Chamberlain. "This must be in strict confidence, Lawrence."

Chamberlain raised his hand. "You can trust my discretion – completely."

Arthur looked towards the tents again and started to speak softly as though to himself.

"Yesterday Hooker fought well, he used his artillery reasonably well and he presented an organised attack. Unfortunately he was wounded and his replacement was not up to the situation. Then incompetence entered - I saw Federal regiment after Federal regiment fed, one by one, piecemeal into the battle in the cornfield against the Confederates, who I don't feel were very strong on the ground." He paused.

"If General McClellan had used his forces, well supported, together with half his reserves, he would almost certainly have swept that field and so turned the Confederate flank. I don't think Lee had anything in reserve. You could see it by the thin bustle of movement just behind their positions." He sipped at his coffee while Chamberlain remained silent.

"It's all very well me being wise after the event," he continued, "and not having the responsibility of an army on my shoulders. I'm sure McClellan had many more factors to consider than my simple view. But Burnside meanwhile was on the left wing." Arthur shook his head. "He was a disaster." After a short pause he continued. "He made all the basic errors of bad generalship. General Burnside did not have his front reconnoitred. If he had done so, he would have found a ford just below his dedicated crossing point, but he fought a basic action of a full division on a twelve-foot front - the width of the bridge! He tried to advance against a superb defensive position that was served by a small number of defenders who were well dug in. It was only by massive bloodletting that Burnside managed to get his division across the Antietam." Arthur took another sip of his coffee.

"To feed regiment after regiment with gaps between their attacks across a single narrow bridge was obscene. And yet gradually the courage of these part-trained volunteer infantry men wore down the defence with their own blood. They won that crossing for this appalling General who ought to be court-martialled and discharged from the army in disgrace."

Arthur then looked straight at Chamberlain. "His worst mistake was that he gave no support to his attack. He did not use his guns or the rifle power of his other infantry regiments. If he had concentrated his very few batteries all onto the entrenched defenders for an hour before the attack, and continued during the attack on the bridge, he could have succeeded earlier with much less loss of life. But no – he started the attack late – with just one battery, on a twelve-foot front, in dribs and drabs. He crossed at 1pm, then delayed for some time and finally moved forward. By this time Lee was able to move his depleted forces to defend the town and also more Southern reinforcements were pouring in. I could see them from where I was on the opposite slope. Burnside was a disaster."

Arthur sipped his coffee then said. "I'm sorry. I have said too much."

"But you have spoken from the heart," replied Chamberlain. "There is never an apology needed for that."

"Thank you, Lawrence," said Arthur. "Talking to you like this has concentrated my thoughts and observations. You've made me put into words a whole jumble of thoughts that were tumbling uncontrolled through my mind. I'm grateful."

"Arthur, right at the beginning you asked me if I knew how many of my men were married and fathers. Why did you ask that?"

"I was just playing for time before I answered your original question, 'How went the day?' Mine was a stupid question to ask. It was just to give me a moment to think how I should reply."

Chamberlain looked straight at Arthur and said, "I don't think that's quite true, is it?"

Arthur shook his head, "No, it isn't." He leaned back in his chair. "In virtually all British regiments of any type the Colonel knows all the details of his officers, most of his senior NCOs and some of the long-service men." He leaned forward and holding his mug in his hands said almost to himself, "Damn. I've got myself in a stupid situation." He looked up at Lawrence. "I must be blunt. Your regiment is not just a large number of men willing to obey your orders but men who are fathers, husbands and sons. What I saw yesterday on the field was the use of men as though they were cattle. Burnside knew that if he poured enough cattle across the bridge, the other side would not be able to reload quickly enough and so General Burnside would win a victory – through the blood of his wasted men.

"All senior officers, like you and me, have to order our men, at some time, to fight in impossible situations but hopefully never knowing that the loss of life is pointless. Battles can be won in many ways; the frontal assault, though essential at times, is not the only path to victory.

"You will do your best, Lawrence, but there will be times when you will anguish as to whether you could have done better and so saved a life or even many lives. It is one of the heavy responsibilities of high command. Unfortunately, some Generals, British as well as American, do not accept it fully."

Arthur put down his coffee mug and abruptly stood up. He held out his hand. "Colonel Chamberlain, I wish you every success and safety to you, and all your men."

Chamberlain also rose and took his hand, "Thank you, Arthur. I hope we will meet again – to talk again."

Arthur saluted and mounted his horse, which Forrester had brought to him.

They rode round to the position that L Battery had been moved to after the battle. Captain Reynolds came across to Arthur as he was dismounting.

"Good to see you, Colonel," he said.

"Thank you, Captain." He handed the reins of his horse to Forrester and said, "I watched your Battery in action yesterday and was impressed at your efficiency. From what I saw you were hotly engaged over the cornfield."

The two men walked towards the Battery tent area. "We were supporting the infantry as they fought across the large cornfield. God, that was a terrible fight." Reynolds looked down at the ground as he walked. "I don't know how may bodies there are out there, but there were gallons of blood shed. It was just terrible," he repeated.

"We were then moved closer towards the cornfield to be able to engage a Rebel battery beyond the Hagerstown Pike. They were about 1000 yards away. We managed to silence them after some 90 minutes. We were lucky in that we hit them hard before they knew it was us doing the damage."

The two men reached the Battery tent, went inside and sat down on two camp seats either side of a table.

"We were just helping an attack on the Dunker Church," continued Reynolds, "when the sharpshooters you saw hit us. It was a good job you did see them as they'd have hit a number of my men before we noticed them. It was all very hectic." Reynolds took off his cap and ran his fingers through his thinning hair. "The Rebs opened up again from the hills over the Pike and we engaged but by then we were running short of ammunition so we had to retire and stock up again. We suffered from the sharpshooters again when we moved but luckily no one was killed or horses hit."

"What were your casualties?" asked Arthur.

"One dead and five wounded."

"You look tired, Captain. When did you last sleep?"

"I'm not sure, sir," replied Reynolds wiping a hand across his eyes. "It was before we started the battle yesterday."

Arthur instantly stood up and moved towards the entrance of the tent. "That's not good, Captain. Please try and get some sleep as quickly as possible. You've done your bit - now leave it to your subordinates."

Reynolds smiled. "I'll take you advice, sir."

Arthur gave a salute to Reynolds before the Captain had time to replace his cap, then left the tent and walked back to where Forrester was holding his horse.

Chapter 7

On the next day General Lee skilfully disengaged his army and withdrew it back across the Potomac River. McClellan, because he was still certain that he had the inferior force, decided not to follow up his attack and so allowed the Confederates to retire without pressure. He remained in the same area for a further three weeks, until President Lincoln visited him at Sharpsburg on October 3rd when he hoped he could get McClellan and the Army moving again, but without success.

After about five weeks of inactivity from McClellan, Lincoln became so infuriated at his lack of initiative and action that he removed him yet again from his senior position commanding the Army of the Potomac and installed General Burnside as the new commanding officer for the Northern Army.

Burnside quickly formed a plan to move towards the Confederate capital of Richmond. He marched his army south and amazingly caught Lee by surprise. Burnside decided that he would swiftly cross the Rappahannock River and attack Lee before he was properly positioned

Rutland's Blues and Greys

with all his army. To do this Burnside needed pontoons to be able to build a bridge across the Rappahannock river near the town of Fredericksburg.

He successfully outwitted Lee and arrived at the town very quickly but unfortunately the instructions to supply the pontoons had been delayed and the flat-bottomed boats needed for the bridge were not available. In fact the Union Army had to wait for more than three weeks before this vital bridge-making material eventually arrived. By that time, Lee had concentrated his army and formed them up in a strong defensive position.

Amazingly, Burnside again did not order any proper reconnaissance to check if the river could be crossed elsewhere. If he had, he would have found that the river could easily be forded upstream and so he would have sprung a great surprise on Lee but, when many days later, Burnside was told that it was possible to cross over, he refused to allow it and insisted that his original plan was adhered to – in detail.

So the Union Army camped on the banks of the Rappahannock and waited for the bridge-building boats to arrive.

While he awaited for the Union Army to arrange their attack, Arthur rode around the various batteries and regiments always with Forrester for company. The two men found a comfortable relationship and talked freely and with ease.

"What will you do after the war, Sergeant?" Arthur asked.

Forrester looked surprised. "After the war, sir?"

"Yes. It won't go on for ever."

"I'm a regular soldier, Colonel."

"No, I don't think you'll stay in the Army. You seem to be a duration soldier to me, not a dyed in the wool regular."

"Duration soldier?" queried Forester.

"Yes. Fight to the end of the war, and then fit into civilian life."

"No, sir. I'm a regular soldier. I signed up before the war started."

"What do your parents say?" asked Arthur.

Forester showed surprise. "My parents?"

"When you write home, don't they query what you are doing?"

"Write home, sir?"

"Sergeant, you are replying to all my questions with another question. 'Write home, sir.' What do they say?"

Forester paused and then said. "I don't write home, Colonel."

"What, never?"

"No, never."

"My goodness," exclaimed Arthur. "I write to my wife almost every evening and then send it as a long letter once a fortnight."

"A fortnight, what's that?"

"Oh, sorry, two weeks, fourteen days is a fortnight," explained Arthur. "Sergeant, you should write regularly to your parents for a number of reasons. They worry about you and want to know you're safe. Then they want to know what is happening here – they've only got newspaper reports to go by. You can tell them what it's really like and what's happening. It's also a discipline that you would benefit from in any career, and, you never know, you might come to enjoy it."

The look on Forrester's face told Arthur that his comments were completely wasted.

"Forgive me, Sergeant, for lecturing," said Arthur. "I just suggest that you could control your own future rather than let it slip into the easy option."

It was on one of these tedious waiting days that Arthur rode down to L Battery, where he always found some point of interest in American life or its handling of the guns. It was stationed with Major General Franklin's Left Grand Division on the left wing of the Union Army, well away from the intended bridge crossing into Fredericksburg.

Arthur dismounted and walked towards the battery officers quarters while Forrester led his horse away. He saw Captain Reynolds leave his office tent and walk towards him. "Good morning, sir."

"Good morning, Captain."

Reynolds had a twinkle in his eye and a smile on his face that surprised Arthur. "At long last we've got a professional artilleryman," he said. "We've got a new Lieutenant, who is a countryman of yours serving with us."

"An Englishman?"

Reynolds turned and looked over towards his guns, then he called out to a young officer. "Lieutenant. Here, please." The young man ran over and saluted the Captain. "You wanted me, sir?"

Arthur noted the British style salute and heard the English voice.

"I think the Colonel here might be interested in you," replied Reynolds then, with a smile, turned and walked back to the battery tent to leave the two Englishmen alone together. The Lieutenant faced Arthur, saw his British uniform and rank, smiled and saluted. "Good afternoon, sir"

"Well, well," said Arthur. "What are you doing here?"

"I wanted to see some action after leaving the Shop."

"My goodness, I didn't expect anyone to call the Woolwich Military Academy 'the Shop' over here. What's your name, Lieutenant?"

"Charles Hastings, sir."

"Where are you from?"

"My home is in Winchelsea in Sussex."

"I know it well. One of the Cinque ports," said Arthur. "And in such beautiful countryside," he added.

"Yes, sir. I certainly miss it."

"How long have you been in America ?"

"Just four weeks. I told the American authorities I wanted to be placed with a battery in action, and here I am."

"Well, Hastings, I'm certain you're in for some surprises with the American way of life and also their method of using guns."

"Have you some words of wisdom for me, sir?"

"Yes. Don't offer any advice or comment unless directly asked for it. They're not especially sensitive but they are doing a number of things incorrectly as we see it and they could well be affronted by any unasked for criticism. I've seen so much that has amazed me but I've managed to keep quiet – just."

"I shall heed your comments, sir," said Hastings. "I'm already amazed that they call me Chuck, which apparently is their diminutive of Charles."

Arthur threw back his head and laughed. "Well, Chuck, it seems you're firmly on the learning stool already." With a smile on his face he turned and walked towards Reynolds at the battery tent while Hastings returned to his guns.

As the days turned into weeks, the waiting was becoming tedious for Arthur so one morning he decided to ride out with Forrester to the right flank and view the countryside well away from the battle scene to be. But that morning, when the Sergeant rode up it was obvious that he was ill. He had either 'flu or one of the other general camp illnesses.

"Go and see the Medical Officer. Tell him that I've sent you there," said Arthur. "I'm going for a long ride well clear of the enemy as I want to see the countryside around. Now off you go."

Forrester pulled his horse's head around and slowly walked it away towards his billet and the medicos.

Arthur decided to ride north, upstream through the village of Falmouth. He followed a track for almost a mile through the heavier timber but still within sight of the river. The sides of the valley gradually got closer to the stream. It was bitterly cold but in the river valley he was reasonably shielded from the cutting icy wind.

Arthur pushed his horse on, and then let it pick its own way down the valley slope to the edge of the river.

There he allowed it to walk into the shallow waters and onto a flat gravel area where the horse nuzzled the water and drank. Through the shallow clear water Arthur could see the bedrocks that spread towards the middle of the watercourse. He slid off his horse and, carefully stepping from stone to stone, ended up standing on a flat rock almost in the middle of the river. He looked at the banks downstream. They were so very similar to the River Wye near Brecon where it ran towards the Black Mountains. Were there trout and even salmon there in season he wondered? He quickly became lost in the beauty of the local countryside.

"Hey, Billy Yank! Are you awantin' to die?" shouted a voice from the far bank.

Arthur jerked himself out of his dreams and into the present. He looked across towards the thick growth on the far side where he thought the voice had come from. Standing in the open as he was, he had only one reply. "No," he called back. "I certainly do not. Are you from the Southern Army?"

"What fool question is that, Yank?" came the reply. "What're y' doin' out there?"

"I was looking at the beauty of the river." He heard a noise of rustling from the bushes as the caller moved closer, plus the mixed sounds of his comments - 'Dang fool'.

Arthur stood perfectly still watching the far bank until a man, scruffily dressed in a worn grey uniform, gradually appeared. His rifle, with bayonet attached, was held at the ready, and pointed at Arthur.

The man, heavily bearded and with a brown slouch hat, slowly approached. His musket point was held at

Rutland's Blues and Greys

the high port but gradually, as he approached, it was lowered to a less aggressive position. When he was on a rock just a few feet away across the shallow stream, he said slowly and suspiciously. "Just who are you, Billy?"

"I am Colonel Rutland of Her Majesty's Royal Artillery."

"You what?" came the explosive reply. "Who's 'her majesty'?"

"Queen Victoria of Great Britain." replied Arthur.

"Well, I'm danged." The man eased the hammer down on his musket lock, and lowered the butt of his gun down onto the rock by his feet. "Are you English?"

"Yes," replied Arthur, and then asked, "Who are you?"

"Me, oh heck, I'm just a sentry posted out here."

"What's your name?" said Arthur.

"I'm Private Dan'l Journay."

"Pleased to meet you," said Arthur and stretched his hand out across the tumbling waters between the two slabs of rock either side of the river. Daniel reached across, just managed to hold Arthur's hand and said, "Pleased to meet you too, Colonel."

"This is a lovely stretch of river," said Arthur. "It reminds me of a river at home."

Daniel nodded and, looking downstream, said, "Yup, it sure is purty." The two men, either side of the river and either side of the battle, stood for a moment to watch the silken flow of water as it swept along.

Daniel broke the silence. "Where're you from, Colonel?"

"I'm from England. I live in Surrey, just south of London."

"Well, pardon me askin', but what are you adoin' here? Are you fightin' for the Yankees?"

"No. I'm just observing what's going on here."

"Observin'. What the spit does that mean? Are you helping the Yankees?"

"No. I'm here to see what's happening and how the war is being conducted."

Daniel looked at Peter in silence, and then he said, "You mean, you ain't fightin'? You's just here to see us fight?"

Arthur was surprised by the phrasing of the question. He had not faced it as bluntly as that, made especially so coming from one of the men actually doing the fighting.

"No. I'm not just here to watch. I'm here to see how the Northern Army uses its cannons in battle. I'm a professional soldier so I want to know the best way of using the tools of my trade."

Daniel leaned on the muzzle of his gun and looked down at the water flowing past his feet. "Well, I dunno," he said slowly. "If I wasn't made to come out here and fight, I surely wouldn't be here just a watchin'. I'd go home." He lifted his head and looked down the river again. "No, I wouldn't want to watch the killin' and woundin' in a battle." Again there was a pause, then looking down at the rocks he said almost to himself, "I'd rather be home with my kinfolk." This honest statement came as a shock to Arthur. Here was the enemy, a man who did not want to kill anyone, or be killed. He just wanted to go home and live the peaceful life he had previously had with his family.

"Where's your family home?" asked Arthur.

"Way down in Georgia. It's just outside of Shingler, in Worth County. Shoot you ain't never heard of it, Colonel."

"No, I haven't. What's it like?"

The Grey paused while he thought about the reply. He had never been asked to describe his own home to anyone before. When he replied, he spoke softly almost to himself as he gazed at the sparkling water at his feet. "It's got soil that'd grow anything, 'n rain to water it, then plenty of sun to ripen it." He lifted his eyes to look at the river further away. "We gotten a creek just like this 'n, 's called Abrams Creek."

"Why are you fighting?" asked Arthur.

Daniel paused again to think. "Well, it's because we made our home patch ourselves and we don't like being pushed around, I guess. Yup. Leave us alone and we're peaceable folks but push us and we can git right ornery. Especially when the gorilla in the White House gets tellin' us what to do."

Daniel stopped, and then looking back at the woods on his side of the river, said, "I shouldn't be atalking to you by rights. I gotta be gettin' back."

"Wait a minute," said Arthur and felt in his jacket pocket for his cigar case. "Would you like a cigar?"

"Well, that's right kindly of you, Colonel. I surely would." Arthur emptied out the five cigars from his case and handed them over to Daniel.

"Mighty grateful, Colonel. The boys'll enjoy these." Carefully holding the cigars, Daniel turned to step across the stones back on his side of the river bank. "Well, Colonel, nice meetin' you," he said.

"And nice meeting you, Daniel," called Arthur.

Daniel stopped, turned and said, "What's your given name, Colonel?"

"Arthur. My name is Arthur."

"Arthur," said Daniel. "Ain't that the name of a king many years ago?"

"Yes. King Arthur."

"He must've been one of yourn. We don't have many kings in our past times."

Arthur watched as Daniel walked back to the bank, where he stopped, turned around and waved.

"Take care of yourself, Daniel," called Arthur.

"You take care as well, Arthur."

Chapter 8

Next morning Forrester reported for duty and he appeared to be much better. Arthur decided that they would walk round to L Battery to see if they knew of any action in the offing. As he strolled along with the Sergeant at his side, Forrester spoke to him in a slightly embarrassed tone.

"Ah, Colonel. I took your advice and wrote to my mother."

Arthur smiled. "Well done, Sergeant."

"But it's turned out rather strange."

Arthur raised his eyebrows in surprise. "Strange?"

"Yes, sir. I wrote to her, with a couple of sketches, and simply explained what life was like here and went on to tell her about Antietam – it took pages."

Arthur smiled and nodded. "When you get stuck in, it always does."

"But she replied, sir."

Arthur showed surprise "Well, why not?"

"But she said that she had sent the letter to a magazine called Harper's, and they had printed most of it – including the pictures."

Arthur threw back his head and laughed. "Bull's eye at first attempt. Well done."

"But they paid for it - and have asked for more."

Arthur gave another loud laugh. "Bravo. Who'd have thought it, a mere Provo Sergeant as a war journalist."

"Should I do more, Colonel?"

"Of course. Maybe this is the step for your new career after the war."

"But I'm writing about the war," said Forrester. "What would I write about when it's ended?"

Arthur swept his arms in a wide arc. "This is an enormous country which has so much to be explored. Your subjects are endless – as long as you seek for them."

The two men approached the battery gun site and Arthur swept his arm in front of him and said, "Just look around you and think about what you see. Don't just accept it - remember it, question it. Then later you will be able to recall so much that you will have plenty to write about. Look at this battery. Look at the men, all from different backgrounds, all with likes and hates - look at the guns, at the equipment, at the weather and the countryside - even at the enemy. If you can write -" he paused, "and sketch," he emphasised, "you are set for a great career. Let the Army keep you while you make yourself known to magazines and papers."

Forrester looked dazed. He was taking in some of what Arthur was saying but was obviously swamped by the rest. Arthur realised this and gave a laugh. "Come on

- first step. Go and see the Gunner Sergeants and look at them closely. I'm going to see Captain Reynolds."

Reynolds was sitting inside his battery tent but came out when he saw Arthur approach. He saluted and said, "Good morning, Colonel. We've just received some supplies of meat which looks a lot better than usual, sir. I wondered if would you join us for dinner this evening?"

"With great pleasure," replied Arthur. "I eat very good food at the Staff mess but the company is not the best. I would very much enjoy eating with you all here."

Reynolds smiled and then he said, "Colonel, at Antietam we could see you very clearly when you were behind us because of the red band on your cap. Do you think it wise to wear such a conspicuous cap, sir?" he asked. "You make a perfect target for a rebel sniper. They don't know that you're not with us. You just look like a high ranking Federal officer."

Arthur nodded. "I suppose you're right but I don't see what I can do about it."

"If you will excuse my effrontery, but I have something for you, sir, that would make me feel easier."

"Make you feel easier?" queried Arthur."

"Yes sir." Reynolds stepped back inside his tent and then came out holding a Union artillery cap with crossed cannons on the top. "If you wore this, you would be just one of us, not a senior one of us."

Arthur took the cap and said, "Captain, I shall be proud to be counted as one of you. My sincere thanks." He held the cap in his hands and facing it towards him he said, "I'll put my Royal Artillery flaming grenade badge on the front." He turned the cap in his hands. He felt embarrassed that Reynolds had made this very understanding gesture. He looked up, smiled, and said, "My thanks again, Captain, for your concern. I am truly grateful."

In the evening, after the dinner of large steaks, Arthur and the three Union Artillery officers sat around the sparkling embers of the open fire that gave warmth and comfort just outside the officers' main tent. They chatted about a range of subjects, all as equals - it was a very pleasant atmosphere. Arthur decided to have one last cigar and then ride back to his billet at Staff HQ. As he threw the stick of his lucifer match into the fire, all four officers heard the beautiful notes of 'Taps' being played by the battery trumpeter.

"Jamieson surely makes it sound beautiful," said Reynolds. "I tell him to always play it twice so that we can truly hear it."

The haunting and emotionally moving sound of the 'end-of-the-day' call floated twice across the artillery park. Everyone stayed still to listen, enjoy and appreciate it. As the last notes drifted away, Arthur lifted his cigar to draw at it and some smoke drifted across his face. With the back of his hand he wiped his watering eyes.

"Well, Colonel, I never expected to see a hardened old soldier like you moved to tears by Taps."

Arthur laughed. "Unfortunately, Captain, this hardened old frame, though moved by that lovely sound, was only reduced to tears by cigar smoke getting in my eyes."

"Don't worry, sir. I won't tell anyone – and smoke in the eyes is a good excuse."

Arthur smiled to Reynolds, and to himself. He felt that he had been accepted into the life of L Battery so well that they could pull his leg. He felt very satisfied.

He rose and said, "Thank you gentlemen for your food and your company but I must now get some rest for this old frame." The officers stood up. Reynolds saluted and said, "Good night, sir."

Arthur walked over to the other camp fire where Forrester was sitting with a group of gunners. He could see the sergeant had a quarto pad on his lap and that he was sketching. Arthur stood behind Forrester, without him knowing, and saw that he was drawing a picture of a gunner who was sitting on a log, smoking a pipe and looking into the fire. It was an amazing picture which in its simplicity showed a battery at rest in camp.

Silently Arthur waited until Forrester, realising that he was being watched, stood up.

Arthur took hold of the pad and looked closely at the drawing. "That is excellent, Sergeant," he said. "Where did you learn how to sketch like that?"

"Learn, sir?"

"You have caught the moment exactly."

"Oh, I just like to draw when I see something of interest, sir."

Arthur nodded and handed the pad back to Forrester. "You're a very lucky man, Sergeant, to have that natural talent. Very lucky."

The bitterly cold weather stayed with the army day and night, which had the advantage of freezing the mud that seemed to be everywhere. Every day Arthur, with Forrester beside him, rode to some part of the army position on the banks of the Rappahannock. He talked to gunners and infantrymen, officers and NCOs and built up an understanding of the men, and the numerous ways that they were different from a British army.

On one of the few sunny days when there was some warmth in the air that was not negated by a cold wind, the two men were riding up a gentle slope of the Stafford Heights towards the Chatham House Headquarters. Arthur noticed a senior staff officer also slowly riding to the crest of the hill; he was slightly ahead and on a parallel track.

"Do you know who that is, Rafferty?" asked Arthur.

Forrester looked carefully at the figure and said, "Ah - that's General Hancock, sir."

Then Arthur remembered he had seen him as a Brigadier General at McClellan's Headquarters before Antietam.

Hancock stopped some hundred yards ahead of them and, from the Heights, looked over the freezing river at the town of Fredericksburg. He took out his glasses and continued his examination as Arthur and Forrester drew level. Arthur could see he was now a two-star Major General.

General Hancock turned to face them and said, "Ah, the British military observer." He paused. "Rutland, isn't it? Colonel Rutland?"

Arthur saluted. "Yes, sir. And impressed by your memory."

Rutland's Blues and Greys

"No, you're not, Colonel. You're a professional soldier and so have a good memory - especially for names, places and faces."

Arthur smiled. He could see now that Hancock was in his late thirties - and cut a handsome figure. Black hair just showed under his hat, while his spiked moustache complemented a trimmed goatee beard. Not for him the flamboyance of mutton chop whiskers or a massive beard.

"So, Colonel," said the General. "As a British Government appointee, you must have been trained in the art of war and be experienced in battle. Where were you trained?"

"At the Royal Military Academy at Woolwich, which for the British artillery is the equivalent of your West Point."

Hancock nodded. "And have you seen battle?"

"Yes, sir. India, Afghanistan and the Crimea. When General McClellan was a military observer."

"Really." Hancock raised his eyebrows. "I didn't know that." He looked back towards the town across the river. "I'm from West Point. But strangely I never made Colonel."

"I beg your pardon, sir?" queried Arthur.

Hancock turned to face him with a smile. "I went from Captain to Brigadier General in one step. I was promoted by General McClellan in July of this year." Hancock looked at Arthur. "Surprised, Colonel?"

"General," replied Arthur. "There have been a great number of surprises for me since arriving here but the elevation of a professional, West Point trained Captain to Brigadier General in one step is one of the easiest surprises to understand. You and your brother officers must be so essential when forming a volunteer army with so many civilian officers in command of even regiments. I met a Professor from Bowdoin College who is now a Lieutenant Colonel and second in command of an infantry regiment. He seems to be a competent man but with absolutely no military training." Arthur stopped wondering if he had said too much, but Hancock looked again at him as though asking for more comment.

"General, I was incredibly impressed at the amazing competence of General McClellan in creating this very efficient Army of the Potomac, and I can well understand that he felt frustrated at not having competent trained professional officers in senior positions - so in answer to your question, General, after some thought I am not surprised at all at your promotion."

Hancock sat in silence looking at the town again. Then he said, "Well, Colonel, you took a long time to get there but I understand what you mean. We have some gifted amateurs but unfortunately some poor-quality professionals."

Still looking over his horse's head at the river, he said, "I expect that your experience of battle has been somewhat different from the type being fought now. I was in the Mexico war which was similar to this but without the newest weapons. The Mexican Army was efficient but the men were paid to fight. Here the men are fighting because they believe." He paused. "I worry that their bravery and willingness to fight comes more from the heart than the head. It is terrifying the faith they have in us senior officers - I do trust we will not let them down." The two men sat on their horses in silence, both lost with their thoughts.

"How long did it take you to get from England to America?" asked Hancock.

"About eight days from Liverpool to New York."

Hancock gently shook his head. "In June my wife and I travelled from California to Washington. I think you travelled only a slightly shorter distance to us but we took weeks and weeks. We came by coach, river boat and railroad. Maybe one day we'll be able to cross all of the way by rail - that will be a wonderful day."

Arthur wondered if he should now leave as the conversation seemed to have stopped. Then Hancock said, "Tell me, Colonel. Do you remember many of the officers you trained with at your Academy?"

"Oh yes, sir. I keep on bumping into them as we all travel around."

"How would you feel if you found yourself actually fighting against one, or a number of them?"

Arthur looked down at his gloved hands that were resting on his saddle and holding the reins. "General, a few days ago I rode up beyond Falmouth and I met a Confederate soldier. We talked and I felt a deep unease at the causes behind this conflict. For me, to find that I was indeed fighting and likely to kill one of my classmates would be a nightmare proposition." Arthur paused, then he softly said, "General, I cannot answer your terrible question." He looked up at Hancock. "Are you in that situation now, sir?"

Hancock gently nodded his head. "In the enemy horde across the river there are a number of men I have served with." He paused, then softly said as almost just to himself. "But there is one especially dear friend out there who I served with in Mexico and California - Lewis, Lewis Armistead. I do pray that no harm comes to him especially from my doing - I wouldn't hurt a hair on his head."

Again there was a silence between the two men. Then eventually the General said, "I must go about my duties now, Colonel. It has been interesting talking to you." He turned his horse to face it back down the slope. "Thank you, sir," replied Arthur as he saluted.

Hancock walked his horse slowly away, all the time looking out across the river.

Forrester walked his horse up to Arthur from where he had been standing a discreet distance away. A freezing flurry of snow blew across the slopes bringing a reminder of the bitter cold that would come in the night as the two men slowly, and in silence, made their way to the Staff HQ.

Eventually the barges for the pontoon bridges started to arrive on horse drawn wagons. It was all very slow and ponderous.

Arthur decided to visit the site of the unloading and set off to ride down to the river bank where, as he happened to pass L Battery position, he heard someone call out to him.

"Like a cup of tea, Colonel?" called a gunner with some sarcasm in his voice.

"No," replied Arthur, "But I'll have a cup of your coffee and a chaw of 'baccy.

The other gunners standing around laughed and one called out, "Hell, Colonel, you ain't never had a chaw of `baccy."

"No," replied Arthur. "and I never will, but I'll have a cup of your coffee when I come back."

"You'll be right welcome," came the reply with a laugh.

Arthur gave a wave of his hand and trotted on, well pleased with the friendly relationship that had been created between him and the men of the battery.

Down at the riverside on the bank directly opposite the town, the pontoons were being unloaded and laid out for use where the bridges were going to be built.

Arthur could see a group of officers around a large pile of planks that presumably were for use as the main road surface across the bridge. He walked over to them and managed to catch the eye of an engineering officer with the shoulder boards of a Captain.

"Excuse me, Captain, where are the bridges actually going to be constructed?" asked Arthur.

"Two will be here, directly across to the town," the Captain replied. " The other three or four will be further downstream. I am only involved with this one."

"Presumably you will have established a foothold over there with infantry before the building," said Arthur.

"I don't think that is arranged, sir." replied the Captain.

"But how will the engineers work? They can't build it under fire from the far bank. They'll all be killed!"

"I'm afraid I don't know, sir."

"Maybe the artillery will be using converging fire from either side of the pontoon on this side to annihilate any enemy on the far bank until the engineers can get the last boat in place," mused Arthur. "My goodness, that is going to be interesting. It'll take very accurate shooting."

The Captain did not reply. He was not aware of anything other than that pontoon bridges were going to be built to get the army across the Rappahannock, which was showing a good covering of ice skimming along on its surface.

In the pitch-dark early morning hours, Arthur was asleep inside his tent when he felt a shake of his shoulder. It was Sergeant Forrester.

"They've started building the pontoons, sir."

Arthur sat up and listened. "I can't hear any artillery firing."

"No, sir. It's very misty outside. I don't think the Rebs know it's happening yet."

Arthur nodded. "Thank you, Sergeant. I'll get dressed and come and see the site."

Forrester left the tent. Arthur threw back his blankets and pulled on his trousers. When he was fully dressed, he pushed through the flap of the tent to see Forrester waiting outside.

"Right, Sergeant, show me where it's all happening."

The two men walked down the slope towards the river, then followed the bank for about two hundred yards. The freezing mist clinging to the surface of the icy river was quite thick and had to be covering the engineers at work. But well before the two of them reached the start of the pontoon works, they could hear the noise of men talking and the boats and lumber being brought to the river's edge.

Rutland's Blues and Greys

The pontoon craft were flat-bottomed barges that were to be lashed side by side and then covered with planks so that the infantrymen could swarm across. Already there were about eight craft lashed together for the first bridge.

Arthur looked around and then walked up the slope and slightly to the side of the work party. He wanted to see the gun sites where the protective cannonade would be fired from. He walked in a semicircle of about two hundred yards radius but could not see any guns. Forrester and he walked back to the pontoon start point where he could see a Major who appeared to be in charge of the work party was standing close to the first barge.

"Excuse me, Major," said Arthur in a low voice. "Where are the support guns situated?"

"Support guns? We haven't any support guns!" he exclaimed. "We'll build the pontoons and the infantry will cross over."

"But surely the Confederates will start shooting at your men soon," said Arthur.

"Well, they haven't so far," he said. Then turned his back on Arthur and walked onto the first pontoon barge to check the work.

"My God!" whispered Arthur. "They'll never make it."

"Make what, sir?" asked Forrester.

"The engineers will never build that pontoon without the Southerners killing them as they approach the other side."

Arthur turned away from the bridge building. "Come on, Sergeant. This is not going to be a healthy place shortly." He strode swiftly up the slope back towards the Headquarters camp with the sergeant trotting quickly behind him to catch up.

It was about two hours later that Arthur heard the sound of rifle fire. The Confederate soldiers, though unable to see the first bridge being built, were firing into the fog towards the sounds of the engineers. The Union men came running back and, though they tried again to work under cover of the mist, the Southern riflemen kept firing at them. It was too much for the engineers to take. Belatedly, General Burnside ordered up artillery to blast the opposite shore to give cover for the engineers.

Arthur wondered what part the guns were playing. Alone they could not keep the Confederate riflemen down because they would have to fire very close to the engineers as they approached the far side.

He was watching the gun at work when he saw that General Hancock was standing close by also watching the battering of the far shore.

Arthur turned to Hancock, saluted, and said, "Is this in preparation for the infantry to cross to make a bridgehead, sir?"

"No, Colonel. This is to clear the Rebel rifle men."

"But after the barrage, surely they'll just return."

"You think so?" asked Hancock.

"Yes, sir."

"We'll see."

When the barrage ended, there was a pause of almost half an hour before the engineers started to recross the half-made pontoon bridge. Arthur could see that General Hancock was again standing a hundred

Rutland's Blues and Greys

yards from the river, with a cluster of officers. They were all watching the men carrying more boards across the bridge - but in only a few minutes, a hail of bullets was fired into the working party from the house ruins on the opposite bank, and the engineers quickly came running back to the Union side.

Arthur looked up at the group of senior officers and saw Hancock turn to face him. The General slowly nodded his head.

Amazingly this bombardment was tried twice more, and each time the Grey riflemen crept out of their hideouts and slaughtered the Blue engineers on the bridge.

Eventually Burnside, in a fit of fury, ordered General Hunt, who was in charge of the artillery, to fire a continuous barrage that would, to all intents and purposes, flatten the whole of the town. It continued for four hours. After half an hour there was a short pause when General Hunt, who was appalled at the destruction, ordered a ceasefire but it was countermanded by Burnside - so the horror continued. The utter wastage of ammunition and the appalling unnecessary damage was, as Arthur knew it would be, a complete waste of time. As soon as it ended, the Rebel infantrymen again crept back to the banks, and from the rubble fired at the working engineers. At last General Hunt's suggestion of sending an infantry regiment across on a number of the pontoon boats to create a bridgehead was agreed on. Arthur watched this and, though it was successful, he was astounded that the crossing infantrymen were still not supported by Union guns firing into the rubble.

This clearing of the far shore allowed the Union engineers to eventually build their pontoon bridge unmolested. A second bridge was quickly added and at long last, after the unnecessary waste of human blood, the Union army was able to cross the Rappahannock and establish themselves in Fredericksburg.

Chapter 9

During all the time that Burnside spent building a crossing over the river, General Lee placed his army in a perfect defensive position - trenches and walls in a line of hills above the town that had connecting roads behind them to move his reserves and supplies safely around the battlefield, well out of sight of the Army of the Potomac.

Downriver of the town his right wing was set back well away from the river and placed in the line of hills that overlooked the Union approach.

The Confederate infantry and artillery on the left wing and the centre, which covered the town and further south, were positioned in layers one behind the other up the long slope to the crest of the hills with the main defence line near the top. The infantry of the far left wing was protected by marshy ground in front that would be very difficult for the Federal troops to cross.

Exactly in the centre, overlooking the town on a hill called Marye's Heights, was a sunken road edged with a stone wall that ran for some 400 yards along the front of the Confederate line. This, though forward of the main defence, was a perfect shield for their riflemen to fire from and, more importantly, it gave excellent protection for them to load their rifles. It stood up to chest high and was a good shield against rifle fire, but it would be vulnerable to shell and shot from the Union guns, which were about 1600 yards away by the river. The Union infantrymen would have to advance five hundred yards up a gentle hill on ground that was completely open. They would be exposed to heavy artillery fire from the guns massed near the crest of the Marye's Heights - all this before the riflemen behind the wall were used.

Burnside had divided his army into three Grand Divisions. The Union Left Grand Division was under the command of General William V Franklin. This would attack below Fredericksburg, crossing the Rappahannock on three pontoons which had been easily built some days before as the ground on the opposite bank was open and without cover for Confederate riflemen.

General Edwin Sumner had the Right Grand Division on the Union right flank. It was his division that would enter the town of Fredericksburg, advance up the slope of Marye's Heights and take the Rebel position.

General Joseph Hooker commanded the Centre Grand Division, which was held as reserve.

Arthur decided that he would follow the fortunes of just one infantry regiment - the 20th Maine. He liked Lawrence Chamberlain and was keen to see how an educated man who had been pushed into a senior military

Rutland's Blues and Greys

position handled himself and his men in battle. Added to this fact, the men of the 20th Maine were as new to battle as their second-in-command and the situation was extraordinary and worth watching. Arthur learned from General Burnside's HQ that the 20th were with General Hooker's Grand Division, which was being kept as a reserve so they were very unlikely to be used in this battle. Arthur smiled to himself with the thought that Lawrence was almost certainly going to be thwarted yet again from fighting and drawing enemy blood for the Northern cause.

Down beside the Rappahannock river, Arthur watched as the Union infantry of General Sumner's Grand Division crossed the pontoon bridge and started to form up in regiments and brigades parallel to the river - and to the Southern lines. After General French's division had crossed, they were followed by General Hancock's division. Arthur and Forrester walked across the bridge into the ruined town of Fredericksburg behind a regiment who showed their origins by wearing a sprig of green in their hats, for they were the Irish Brigade. They were all tough fighting men, led by General Meagher, a true Irishman, who had an 'undying hatred of the English'. He was dressed in a magnificent, tailored green uniform with a yellow silk band across his chest. Though he had been wounded in the knee at Antietam, he was determined to take his 'bhoys' up the slope and be the first to bring the vital breakthrough.

As Arthur and Forrester walked across the bouncing pontoon bridge, the sergeant asked, "Are those rebel guns up there on the hills, sir?"

Arthur shaded his eyes and said, "Yes. A goodly array of them it seems."

"Could they hit this bridge now, sir?"

Arthur again looked carefully and judged the distance. "It would be very difficult at that range."

"Could they bring guns closer to hit it though, sir?"

"Oh yes, that wouldn't be difficult."

"Then why aren't they doing it, sir. Surely they want to stop us crossing, or do they want us on this side of the river?"

Arthur walked in silence. He was deep in thought. "That is a very perceptive question, Rafferty. Why are they letting us cross unmolested?" He walked on still considering the point. Ahead he could hear the thunder of the Southern guns slamming out their shot but not at the bridge - then it was all added to by the ripple of rifle fire. Someone was getting it hot in front.

Having got over the pontoon bridge, Arthur, with Forrester close behind, moved out of the town over to the right to a position where he could see the Union regiments start to form up before advancing up towards Marye's Heights. To his amazement, he could see a wide ditch or small canal some 30 foot wide that ran just in front of the regiments; they would have to cross it before advancing up the slope towards the Southern infantry. He saw General Hancock staring at the forming regiments belonging to the leading Division under General French.

Arthur walked up to him and saluted. "How are the infantry going to cross the ditch, sir?"

Rutland's Blues and Greys

Hancock did not return Arthur's salute but turned with fury in his face. "There is no ditch there to cross, sir. Our General assures us that, despite the reports, there is no ditch to cross. It is not on his map so the regiments will have no trouble in crossing the ditch that is not there, Colonel." He turned abruptly and walked back towards the ruined town.

Arthur was astounded. Burnside was refusing to believe the obvious. The regiments would not only be held up in the face of enemy artillery fire, they would be concentrated together when they crossed the three light wooden bridges from which the planks had been removed and only the stringers were left. The Union attackers would have to carefully and slowly cross over these thin bridges and so become excellent targets. It was to be slaughter yet again.

Arthur could hear orders being shouted for the advance, and then he saw the lines of the next regiment of Union infantrymen, in their dark blue uniforms covered by their heavy overcoats, move across the narrow beam bridges and into the open field beyond. Then the guns of the Southern artillery started and with ease they fired shot and shell into these forming lines as the Union infantry slowly moved forward.

"There is your answer, Rafferty," said Arthur. "There is the field of death on which General Lee has decided he'll slaughter the Union Army. He wants the Yankees to come to him right here - here where he has a magnificent defensive position and a perfect killing area."

Arthur watched from the protection of the shattered buildings in the town as General French's brigades start ed their attack. The first of the obstacles the Union men encountered was the canal, and there they formed into groups to slowly cross the waterway. All the time the Southern cannon continued their deadly fire which tore the regiments to bloody shreds as the gallant men moved forward. Then they found that there were lines of fences that they had to pull down, while all the time the Confederate artillery slammed into the crowded ranks. Eventually, having cleared their path, they moved up the start of the slope.

A short respite came as they reached a slight depression that formed dead ground to hide them from the guns. Then they advanced. Strongly and with purpose, they ran forward in straight regimental lines with fixed bayonets and an ongoing cry of 'Hi Hi Hi'. The glint of their bayonets in the winter sunshine gave them the effect of a stream of blue and steel.

Again the Southern artillery tore into this brave mass as they moved even closer until yet another slight depression in the field gave them some cover. This was enough to straighten lines and fill the gaps until the mass again charged. But Armageddon on a massive scale was inevitably reached as the men neared the stone wall. The Rebel riflemen, who had been waiting for that very moment, stood up to the wall and unleashed a torrent of bullets, firing them straight into the massed ranks of Blue soldiers.

The Union men fell in droves. Gradually the impetus of their charge withered and the pitiful survivors staggered back to the comparative shelter of the depression. Their charge had failed.

The next brigade was following close behind, and they repeated the deadly path of their companions only to fall to the same storm of lead and shell until they also turned and ran. The third brigade followed into the path with the same bloody results.

Arthur watched in horror at this terrible waste of human life. He could see General Hancock standing in front of massed infantry which was the lead brigade of his Division, who Arthur felt were simply being led as sheep to the slaughter.,

Behind the lead brigade came the Irish. Arthur, with Rafferty in tow, followed beside these men into their start position. The Irish Brigade came by with their evergreen sprigs stuck in their hats. Proud, defiant and irresistible! The Irish men were singing and showing the cocksureness of seasoned warriors.

As they started to cross the canal and the shells fell amongst them, Arthur and Rafferty also crossed the canal.

"We shouldn't be here, sir," shouted Forrester.

"I want to go just a little closer to see where the guns are."

As Arthur walked beside the end rank of the Irishmen, he realised that, though bravery was obvious, some of these men were terrified. He saw a young man, almost a boy, on the outside rank striding up the slope in line with his comrades. He was staring ahead and murmuring something to himself. As the soldier came closer, Arthur could hear the lad saying "Hail Mary, full of grace. Hail Mary, full of grace." He was repeating this line of the Rosary again and again to himself - but would his God keep him safe? "Hail Mary, full of grace. Hail Mary, full of grace."

But both Arthur and the lad knew that his chance of being alive in an hour's time was remote to impossible.

Arthur stopped at the edge of the first field and watched the Brigade move forward. After a hundred yards or so the regimental lines moved into the slight dip and into the dead ground where the Confederate riflemen could not see them. Then as the Blue ranks emerged for the charge up the hillock towards the stone wall, yet again the Greys raised their rifles over the edge and poured their rifle fire into the concentrated lines of Blue.

As the Irish advanced up the slope, they seemed to lean forward as though they were pushing against heavy rain or into a strong wind but they were facing a deadly storm of bullets that inevitably tore them apart.

Regimental and National colours fell, were picked up to be carried a few more paces before falling again, and yet again picked up. Gradually the ranks thinned from men dropping down wounded and dead until the advance stopped some fifty yards short of the stone wall from where the rebels continued to pour Minie bullets into the advancing Northerners. But the Irish Brigade never stood a chance - they broke and ran back towards the ditch.

Arthur was horrified at this appalling use of flesh to counter bullets. Where was the artillery support? He looked around. It might not be possible to bring a battery into action just here but there must be somewhere that the line of sight would be directly at the stone wall. But there were no guns in sight. Apparently none had crossed the pontoon bridges so the infantry were expected to take the slopes without any support - just like Burnside's attack at Antietam.

Arthur looked over to his right. Was it not possible to move men over there? But as he looked through his glasses, he could see the shine of water on the fields. They were just marshes with the slurry of a bog. A veritable slough of despond.

He turned and the two of them walked back over the bloody, corpse-filled canal and through the wrecked town towards the river. 'Surely guns could be used from the other side of the river?' he thought. Mentally he carefully measured the distance from the river bank to the stone wall. It had to be about 1600 yards. L Battery's 3-inch rifle guns would have been able to handle that!

As they walked back through the smoking ruins of the town, they could see another brigade was being brought up to attack. These infantrymen had not yet seen what had happened before, so they had no idea to what they could expect but Arthur and his Sergeant knew what hell awaited these men.

Behind this Union mass there were more regimental lines gradually forming. Methodically, line by line, regiment by regiment, brigade by brigade, they were fed into the slaughter machine until the grassy slopes in front of the stone wall on Marye's Heights was covered in mounds of Blue. Some still in death, others writhing in the agony of wounds, and a few trying to crawl back to some sort of cover.

Where was the Union artillery support? Arthur looked around. It would have been difficult to get a clear line of fire but not impossible. So the Greys, who were well sheltered behind the stone wall, just loaded and fired. Their losses were minute in comparison to the slaughter of the Union infantry.

Arthur turned and started to walk down Hanover Street back towards the pontoon bridge. Dusk was only an hour or so away as he neared the river edge. He was going to recross the pontoon bridge when he saw the tall figure of Lawrence Chamberlain standing beside the Regimental commander, Colonel Ames, in front of the 20th Maine Regiment that was waiting for its turn for the attack. So Burnside was throwing in his reserves against an enemy defensive position that had already smashed his Right Grand Division.

Arthur stopped and put out his arm in front of Forrester to hold him back. They both stepped back off the road and out of the obvious view of Chamberlain. Arthur wanted to look at this man who had given up his career of teaching in a prestigious College to come and fight for his country and its cause. A dedicated, thinking man who was ready to lay down his life for his standards - and he was about to be called for this final sacrifice.

Arthur looked at Lawrence's profile with his drooped moustache. The man was calm and ready. He was no fool, so he knew that death was a great probability if not a certainty, but he was standing as steady as a rock for his men who were about to die with him.

Arthur watched the regiment and its commanders for some time until eventually the order was given for the 20th Maine to advance. As they marched off, he stepped out onto the road with Forrester and they both walked back over the pontoon bridge to the main Union camp.

Back in the Union lines Arthur said to Forrester, "Go back to your billet. Come back here tomorrow morning."

The Sergeant frowned. "Is that it, sir? Is the battle over?"

"No, the fighting will start again tomorrow and more will die."

"But how about our wounded lying on the field out there?"

Arthur looked at Rafferty's face, then bowed his head and turned away.

"What about them, sir? They'll die in the cold if nothing's done!"

Arthur could not speak. He continued to walk towards his tent.

"Will nothing be done, sir?" called Rafferty, louder and with terrible anxiety. "Surely they can't... just be left ... to die." His voice slowly faded away.

Arthur carried on walking until he reached his tent, pulled back the flap and went in. He dropped his hat on his camp bed and sat down on the edge. He felt so depressed at the appalling example of leadership and he knew he would not sleep much that night knowing, just like Rafferty, that so many wounded and dying men were still out on that slope of death.

Chapter 10

Next morning Arthur woke and stepping out of his tent saw the freezing fog that covered the river valley. He slammed his arms around himself to start up some circulation and get some warm blood moving through his body. He walked through the frozen grass to the HQ Staff mess, where he found some coffee and a couple of hard-tack biscuits that he munched as his breakfast, then he returned to his tent to put on his heavy caped overcoat. Surprisingly, Forrester was not waiting at the tent as was usual. Arthur looked around but there was no sign of the Sergeant so he decided to walk down to General Hooker's HQ to find out what had happened to Chamberlain and the 20th Maine.

Through the cold and foggy air, across the ice-hardened mud, he strode down to the river where Hooker's HQ was situated. As he approached the main tents, he heard a stamping and puffing behind, and turning round saw Forrester stumbling towards him.

"I'm sorry I'm late, sir." Forrester was a muddled mess. His uniform looked as though it had been thrown on, while his face was drawn and a sickly yellow.

"You look awful, Sergeant. Do you feel ill?"

Forrester tried to adjust his jacket and belt. "No, sir. I'm fit, it's just that....."

"Just what, Sergeant?"

"I got drunk last night, sir." Forrester was still trying to smarten himself up as Arthur watched and gradually understood.

"It was all so terrible, sir. I had to do something." Forrester lowered his head and his voice. "So I got drunk."

Arthur nodded his head in understanding. "Alright, Rafferty. Go back to your billet, clean up and get some sleep."

"Oh, no, sir. Please let me come with you. I can't bear to be alone."

Arthur smiled and then reached out to adjust Forrester's cap on his head. "You still look awful, so stay in the background, that's all."

"Thank you, sir."

Arthur opened the flap of the Staff tent and entered to see a number of officers inside, some of whom were standing in front of a map pinned to an easel.

One of them, a Colonel, turned to Arthur and abruptly said, "Yes?"

"Can you tell me where I can find the 20th Maine and especially Colonel Chamberlain?"

The Union Colonel turned to another officer and then came over to stand close to Arthur.

"As far as we know, the 20th Maine is still on the far slope." He paused. "Lieutenant Colonel Chamberlain is amongst the casualties and is almost certainly dead."

Arthur felt this was the answer he had expected. "Thank you," he replied and walked out of the tent.

Outside he stood a few paces away from the entrance. Then slowly and softly he swore. "Damn, Damn, Damn."

Forrester, who had been waiting close by, came up and stood in silence at Arthur's side. He knew it was the worst news, and that his Colonel was taking it badly.

Arthur raised his head and, looking myopically into the foggy air, he said, almost in a sob, "Oh God."

Rafferty gently put his hand on Arthur's shoulder to share the anguish that they were both feeling.

Arthur looked at Forrester and said, "Come on, Rafferty. Let's go and see Captain Reynolds and his gunners."

It was a long walk from the centre pontoon down to the crossing for the Left Division, and the two men walked in utter silence - both surrounded by their thoughts which, though the same, were not to be talked about.

The mood in the gun park was as depressed as it was in the rest of the Union Army.

Captain Reynolds saluted Arthur, but there was no smile on his face. "Were you with the right flank sir?"

"Yes, Captain, but to be brutally honest I don't want to talk about it. What happened here with you?"

Reynolds took off his cap and ran his hand through his thinning hair. "The Battery was moved back and forward, sometimes coming into action under fire,

Rutland's Blues and Greys

sometimes not knowing what our target was, and sometimes taking on Rebel batteries. I had to leave the command to my brother Gilbert as I was called away to be Brigade Chief of Artillery due to casualties. If only we had a central command for the artillery."

"You're still under control of infantry regiments as they want assistance?" queried Arthur.

Reynolds nodded. A messenger ran up to Reynolds, saluted and gave him a note. The Captain read it and said to Arthur, "Excuse me, sir. I'm wanted at Headquarters." He saluted and followed the messenger across the gun park.

Arthur looked around at the rest of the gun park and saw Lieutenant Hastings walking slowly back to the Battery Command tent. Hastings noticed Arthur, walked over and saluted. His face was tired and solemn.

"You were absolutely, sir." he said. "They do things differently here."

Arthur nodded. Then Hasting let his feelings pour out. "They just don't understand how to use guns. It was terrible. We were moved from one place to another and then we ran out of ammunition so I was sent back to get restocked. It was then that I saw what was happening in the fight beyond the town up against that stone wall. Where were the guns, sir? Where were the bloody guns?" He bowed his head in despondency.

Arthur put his hand on Hastings' shoulder. "You are right. It was appalling."

Hastings slowly shook his head. "I don't think I can stay here now."

Arthur spoke abruptly. "You must stay, Lieutenant. For your own sake and for the Union Army. You will be promoted at some time - they're very short of officers, especially gunnery officers and certainly trained ones. You must stay."

Hasting looked up at him. Arthur again put his hand on Hastings' shoulder. "Charles, they need you. They don't know it yet but they will need you."

Hastings nodded his head. "Thank you, sir, you're right. I will stay - but it's hard, damned hard."

Arthur turned away and walked out of the gun park 'Yes,' he thought. 'It is damned hard.'

It was not until late in the afternoon the second day that the Union Army, under a mutual truce, started to return from across the Rappahannock with its terrible number of wounded.

Arthur stood with Forrester by the pontoon and watched the slow column of troops returning across the river. Suddenly he realised that the senior officer amongst them was Lawrence Chamberlain. Arthur in amazement called out, " Lawrence !"

Chamberlain turned a weary and mud-stained face towards him. Arthur pushed through the soldiers to walk alongside him and said, "I beg your pardon, Colonel, but I am so delighted to see you. I'd heard that you were dead on the field."

Lawrence wearily nodded as though in a trance. "I thought I was dead as well, but the Good Lord saw fit to spare me."

"Is your brother Tom safe as well?"

Chamberlain nodded. "Yes, Tom's well," he said. "But you know, Arthur, we could have made it. With just a few more men, we could have taken that wall."

The comment sent a shock wave of horror through Arthur. After all that this man had seen, he still held the belief that his senior General had acted correctly and the Union could have won the day.

"No, Lawrence," said Arthur in a low tone. "You would never have passed the wall."

Chamberlain opened his mouth to disagree, but Arthur raised a hand to silence him. "You didn't see but behind that stone wall, and to your right, there was line upon line of Confederate infantry ready for you. They never fired a shot because you were being beaten in front of the stone wall." He paused. "No one would ever have taken that position."

As the men walked out of the town and across the bridge to return to the Union position, the early night sky swiftly transformed into an amazing swirl of dancing lights and clouds. It was an incredible and unbelievably beautiful display.

"What is that?" exclaimed Arthur gazing up at the swirling streams of lights that seemed to boil across the sky. Chamberlain smiled wearily. "We see them quite occasionally up in Maine. It is the aurora borealis, but I doubt if it is seen much down here. They are called the Northern Lights." He lowered his gaze and slowly continued to walk back to his regimental lines with the few men he had left.

It was much later that day when Arthur and Forrester left the river and returned to the L Battery gun park.

Captain Reynolds was standing by the Command tent with a couple of grips beside him.

He saluted Arthur and said, "Well, sir, I am now going to be permanently with the Brigade, and my brother Gilbert is replacing me as L Battery Commander."

"Congratulations, Captain. I hope the someone who decided you should be there also decides to promote you." Reynolds smiled in response.

Behind the Captain, Arthur could see a knot of officers coming down the road. The way they were grouped, it looked as though the one in front was a senior officer. "Who's this?" he asked.

Reynolds turned round. "General Hunt. He is the Chief of Artillery," he said and saluted as the group approached. Arthur also gave the courtesy of a salute to a senior officer.

The group stopped and Reynolds walked over to the leading man and again saluted. They spoke for a few moments and then the Captain came over to Arthur. "General Hunt would like to talk to you, Colonel."

"To me?" queried Arthur. "Very well." He walked smartly over and saluted the General.

"Colonel Rutland, sir."

Hunt returned the salute and looking down from the saddle said, "The Captain says you are an English observer from the British Artillery."

"Yes, sir."

"Presumably you send your observations back home after we have viewed them."

"Exactly, sir."

"Well, Colonel, as I've not seen any of your reports, please tell me what you think of our use of artillery."

Arthur was stunned. He stood in silence as he tried to work out a non-committal answer that was not patronising. General Hunt gestured to his ADC and dismounted. The ADC took his horse's reins.

Hunt came over to Arthur. "Colonel, walk with me, will you, please?"

General Hunt was a stockily built man of medium height. He had a full beard, but it was only a couple of inches long. His dark eyes were set above pronounced bags that gave him a melancholy appeara nce. He walked towards the line of guns where a few gunners were standing. Reynolds instantly waved to the men to leave the guns so that the General and Arthur could speak privately.

"I presume, Colonel, you have difficulty in giving a completely honest answer to me because you feel it might be taken as criticism." Again Arthur did not answer as Hunt was exactly right.

"Well, Colonel, I would like to hear your opinion, good or bad. Firstly, which battles have you observed at?"

"Antietam and Fredericksburg, sir."

"Right. What did you see at Antietam ?" asked Hunt. "And I want an honest answer."

Arthur faced the General, who was looking across the river, and said, "I was on the Federal right wing from the start of the battle. The Confederate guns situated on Nicodemus Heights to the west of the cornfield were well placed and used with skill. They were ranged at some distance of about 700 yards and did considerable damage to the Federal infantry. Union guns to the east, behind the east woods, were used quite well at a good distance but surprisingly left the field after a comparatively short time, having used all their available ammunition. Apparently there was no facility to restock these batteries with ammunition during the battle, so they withdrew.

"At least one battery, B Battery 4th US, came in to action within 50 yards of the Confederates and, though they did amazing work, they suffered completely unnecessarily because they were much too close and subject to easy infantry fire. Having said that, their presence held the line."

Hunt asked "And in the centre?"

"I was not able to see any real use of artillery there as I had moved from the right flank round to the left flank and to the lower bridge."

Arthur paused. "And what did you see there, Colonel?" asked Hunt.

Arthur did not reply at once, then he said, "A disaster, sir. An attack on a narrow front, with little or no artillery support, that led to horrendous casualties with the infantry. I could not see one battery in use giving covering fire. If a couple of batteries had been used for an hour to swamp the entrenched infantry, the bridge could have been taken easily and much earlier. Even rifle fire from Union infantry regiments could have been used during the attack but it was not."

The General did not query Arthur's comment but added another question. "And what about Fredericksburg ?"

"In my opinion sir, good covering fire was given to General Meade's attack on the left flank. If it had been greater, I think that the Confederates might even have been broken but that is just conjecture. The bridging of the river was an unmitigated disaster. The engineers were slaughtered because they were not given proper covering fire before or during their work. Then, when the decision was taken to destroy the houses fronting the river, the bombardment went on far too long, especially as it could have been used while the actual bridge building was being done. It was an appalling misuse of gunnery power."

Arthur was amazed to see Hunt was actually nodding.

"I'm afraid, sir, I leave the worst to last. The fact that there was virtually no gunfire brought to bear on the stone wall on Marye's Heights was in my opinion obscene." General Hunt sharply lifted his head and looked straight at Arthur but did not say a word.

"That those infantry men, one regiment after another, should continue to attack up that slope against a well-protected enemy, who had not felt any artillery shot or shell, was in my mind criminal."

The General said nothing. He simply looked straight ahead, then he faced Arthur.

"Colonel Rutland, thank you for your obviously honestly felt comments. I'll not say whether I agree or disagree but I appreciate your very independent views." With that he held out his hand. Arthur shook it and then saluted the General.

Hunt looked at him. "It was your salute that made me note you." He smiled and walked back to the group of officers, mounted his horse and rode on down the road.

Arthur returned to Reynolds and said, "Well, that was amazing. He asked for my opinion and he took it all without comment. Why did General Hunt want to hear my criticism of his use of guns?"

"Because, sir," replied Reynolds, "though he is known as the Chief of Artillery, he does not instruct us unless we are permitted to act through either our divisional commanders or General Burnside. So General Hunt is Chief of Artillery in name only and almost powerless. He is only used to get us supplies."

"You mean that the infantry commanders can override the orders of the Chief of Artillery?"

Reynolds nodded.

"That is terrible," said Arthur "But it explains a great deal."

Arthur knew that he would have to write a full and detailed report that would be very controversial with the Federal Army and so he decided that he would return to Washington to ensure it could be produced with care and properly submitted.

When he told Forrester, the Sergeant replied, "I've been told, sir, that when you leave, even temporarily, I'm to be posted back to the Provost and moved away. If possible, sir, while I'm waiting for you to return, I would like to be transferred to the guns to stay with L Battery and serve with Lieutenant Hastings, sir."

"Fine. I will inform your Provost commander that I want you available for my needs."

"Actually sir, I have talked to Captain Reynolds about it and he says that though he'd be pleased to have me, he couldn't keep me as a sergeant as he has a full number of sergeants."

"Rafferty, you will learn that in any army there's always a way to get what you want. It is just a matter

Rutland's Blues and Greys

of working the system. You will stay with L Battery because gunner volunteers are wanted. You will stay a sergeant because you are on my staff. I couldn't possibly have a private soldier as an assistant. I must have at least a sergeant."

Forrester smiled. "I think you're very cunning, sir."

"There is no point in getting old without learning some tricks."

As the Army of the Potomac licked its wounds and crossed back over the Rappahannock, General Burnside started to create another plan of attack, but Arthur was not prepared to wait for it to come to fruition.

At L Battery gun park he said goodbye to Hastings and to Forrester. As he was just about to leave the Sergeant came up to him and said,

"I'm sorry to ask for another favour, sir," he said. "But I wondered if you could help me."

"Certainly," replied Arthur. "What's the problem?"

"Well, my mother's still receives money from Harper's for my letters and sketches but she's worried about all the cash in the house. No one uses a bank because they don't trust them but she is worried about the cash being stolen."

"Put it all in a big bank who'll look after it all for you."

"But which bank and how, sir?"

Arthur paused to think and then said, "I'll give you a letter to send to a friend I have in Baltimore, a Mr Hiram Eaves. Send your mother's address to him and I am sure he'll know the best bank to use. You want one where you can get money from them or another bank wherever you are in America."

"Thank you, sir," said Rafferty with obvious relief in his voice.

"It's a pleasure to help a budding author," replied Arthur with a smile. "Make sure you stay with L Battery and I'll catch up with you when I get back in a few weeks' time."

Chapter 11

Life in Washington especially over the Christmas period was a blissful change to the horror and hardships of life with the Army of the Potomac. Arthur took his time with his meticulous reports.

It was just after the New Year of 1863 that Arthur received through the Legation a message from Hiram Eaves asking if he could possibly come to visit them some time later that month. He telegraphed back that he would be able to get away in mid-January, and a reply came from Hiram asking him to a dinner party on January 14th 1863 in Baltimore.

Due to a delay on the railroad, Arthur arrived at the Eaves house rather later than he intended, which meant that he was changing for dinner as the other guests arrived. Eventually he came downstairs and saw Hiram waiting in the entrance hall. "I'm so sorry, Hiram, for delaying you like this."

"Don't worry, Arthur. Come on in and meet the rest of the party."

Hiram led him into the main sitting room, where he was introduced to the other guests, who were Andrew Whelan, a local industrialist, and his wife, Penelope, plus Hiram's brother Carter and his wife, Victoria, whose brother had just been killed at Fredericksburg. She was an attractive woman in her forties with light blond hair and hazel eyes. She was dressed sombrely in a dark grey dress presumably in deference to the loss of her brother. During the evening she appeared to be naturally subdued, but Arthur had a feeling that she was antagonistic towards him and certainly would not allow herself to become involved in any mutual conversation.

Arthur was also surprised that Abigail, though obviously delighted to see him, was not her usual sparkling self that he had known on the ship. It was as though she had some great worry to carry.

During the meal Hiram said to Arthur, "I've had a letter from a Sergeant Forrester who I understand you suggested I could help."

"Did he ask about a bank?" asked Arthur

"Yes. What's it all about?"

"Forrester is an amazing young man who is a dab hand at doing clear and precise sketches. He has also found he's quite good at writing descriptive articles which Harper's are willing to buy."

"Good grief!" exclaimed Hiram. "And he is earning enough to put money in the bank?"

"Definitely," replied Arthur. "His mother is putting all he earns in a tin under the bed or something like that, but she is getting worried about the amount there. I would be grateful if you could help him."

Rutland's Blues and Greys

"Of course. In fact I have already arranged an account with the City Bank of New York. I expect he wants a good bank that'll be able to let him have money wherever he is. He'd be able to use letters of credit on banks in the cities he visits."

"Many thanks, Hiram. I think he has a good future as a writer-cum-artist - as long as he doesn't get killed."

Hiram nodded in understanding.

The meal had finished and the guests were waiting for Abigail to suggest that the ladies should leave the gentlemen alone to smoke and talk men's talk, when Victoria spoke in a firm voice that could be clearly heard by all seated around the table.

"I would appreciate it, Colonel Rutland, if you would tell me how you can come to America just to watch our young men kill each other."

" Victoria !" exclaimed her husband, Carter. "That is not …"

But Arthur raised his hand to Carter. "Please let her continue."

"You're a soldier who knows how to kill. Why do you have to come here?" she said. "Do you enjoy watching our soldiers die? Will you show us how to kill each other more efficiently?" She paused and then she added, "Don't you feel ashamed?" Tears ran down her face as she stopped to take a kerchief from her reticule.

Again Carter spoke. "Arthur, you don't have to answer this..."

"Yes, I do," replied Arthur. "I have to try and answer it now, for Victoria's sake - and for my own."

In the stunned silence, no one at the table moved or said anything - but they were all surprised by Arthur's comment. They waited in the taut and embarrassed atmosphere.

" Victoria, you are right. I am starting to feel ashamed." He looked down at the stem of his wine glass that he held in his right hand. "I'm a Regular Army officer who has fought battles for the past twenty years or so. I've always fought against other professional soldiers in India, Afghanistan and the Crimea. All these soldiers were fighting because they were trained to fight, and because their king, emperor, or ruler said they must. The soldiery were well trained to act to orders but they were, by and large, illiterate. They were soldiers because they chose to be, often because it was their only chance of regular food, clothing and accommodation. They trusted their officers and obeyed them without question. The officers were mainly well trained at leadership and in military manoeuvres.

"Either side was there to hold, or gain land, to protect trades or punish wrongs made by others. To fight any of these battles successfully, it is essential for me, and my brother officers, to know the best way of winning them. This generally means the preservation of lives of our soldiers at the cost of the enemy."

He paused and again looked intently at his wine glass still held between his fingers.

"So it should be with my posting here, but two factors have made me very worried about my position. Firstly, this is a war in which both sides are using incredibly efficient weapons that can kill men quickly, and at long distances – rifles and artillery. Yet the old-

Rutland's Blues and Greys

fashioned method of fighting with men in blocks and ranks is still being used. Now, slaughter is not only easy, it appears to be essential. If an enemy is sending hundreds of men against you, you must kill as many as possible as quickly as possible or you are going to be killed yourself.

"I have seen sights here in just two battles, Antietam and Fredericksburg, that have horrified and sickened me. Rushes of men being used to soak up the enemy ammunition then, when the enemy bullets run out, the remaining Federals charge and win the day. This is an exaggeration but it is basically true."

Again he paused. The silence was tense as all the other guests hung on his every word.

Softly he started talking again. "The second point is to me the most traumatic. These men, Blues and Greys, who are fighting each other, are from one nation but simply with different ideals. The basic soldier or gunner that I meet is a man who can read and write, who would rather be at home but is willing to fight and die for his country or even state. Yet, as far as I can see, the difference between the soldiers on either side is not very great but whatever it is, I do not understand it.

"A few days before Fredericksburg I spoke to a Confederate Soldier who could have shot me but instead he talked to me while we watched the flow of the water in the Rappahannock."

Hiram almost exploded. "You spoke to a rebel?"

Arthur nodded. "He was an ordinary man who was fighting to protect his homeland from Federal invasion. He too was astounded that I was there to watch the fighting. He told me that all he wanted to do was go home, and that he would as soon as Bobby Lee whipped the Yanks."

"But, but.." started Hiram.

"No, Hiram, there is no 'but'. This is a terrible and bloody war - but it seems that pride on both sides has made it inevitable. Now hundreds more men on both sides will have to die before it eventually ends."

Arthur lifted his head, looked at Victoria and spoke directly to her. " Victoria, I'm truly sorry about your personal loss, and, honestly, I can understand your criticism of my position. I do hope that I've not offended you by my presence at this table. Please be assured that I do not give advice or assistance to either side – but I'm not sure how much longer I can carry on with my informed position of not becoming involved. I'm finding it more and more difficult to watch the slaughter of these fine young men, both Blue and Grey, then simply walk away, write a report and end the day by having a good night's sleep."

Victoria, with her head bowed, softly whispered through her tears, "Thank you, Arthur. And I apologise for my harsh tone earlier."

"Please, dear lady," replied Arthur gently. "You have nothing to apologise for."

A silence settled around the table. It was eventually broken by Abigail, who said, "I think that we ladies should now leave the gentlemen on their own."

Everyone stood up and the ladies walked out of the dining room, leaving the four men to re-seat themselves at the table.

Hiram offered cigars from a table humidor that was passed around the table, and the wine glasses were refilled.

"Tell me, Colonel," asked Whelan. "Am I right that you, as an independent observer, think that the North will win?"

"There is no question," replied Arthur. "You cannot be stopped, and eventually the South will plain run out of men – and supplies. The war will drag on for a lot longer because the Confederates have some excellent Generals in Lee, Jackson and Johnston, all of whom are supported by trained Generals under them. The Union have yet to find their mastermind. God knows they need him badly, and quickly."

"Arthur," said Hiram. "You sound scornful of our Generals."

"I think I'm right in saying that all of your senior officers are West Point trained – so they are well educated and efficient but in the past two battles I have only seen one with any flair." Arthur drew on his cigar. "General McClellan has shown himself to be an excellent organisational leader but obviously Lincoln considers him to be much too cautious. While Burnside is so textbook controlled that Lee can predict his every action.

"I am a gunner and therefore biased but the Union Army has forgotten how to use artillery to its best advantage. There is just one man, General Hunt, who is working against incredible bias to drag your artillery into the modern age. At Antietam and Fredericksburg, steady pounding by your superior guns could have won the battles without doubt. The main gun with the Union forces is the smooth-bore Napoleon firing a 12-pound shell at up to 800 yards! The 3-inch rifled gun can fire a 9-pound shell up to two miles! These are the weapons that can discomfort a protected enemy in trenches."

"But, Colonel," exclaimed Carter. "All your suggestions would mean battles taking much longer to complete and enormous problems with the carting of all the necessary ammunition and supplies."

Arthur nodded. "You are quite right - but regarding time, does that matter? I don't think so. At Fredericksburg the Federal Army took days before they lost the battle. The North has the amazing manufacturing ability to produce all the extra shells and hundreds of wagons to carry them."

The conversation flowed between the men for some time until they had finished their cigars and eventually joined the ladies.

Next morning Arthur rose, dressed and then had the usual enormous American breakfast with Hiram in the dining room. Afterwards, he went back to his room, where he packed his valise. He came down the stairs again and, now wearing his caped overcoat, he was ready to catch the train and return to his lodgings in Washington. He stood in the front hall waiting to say his farewells to his hosts when, from the direction of the sitting room, he could hear voices that were raised. Not shouting, just talking slightly louder than usual. It sounded as though Abigail and Hiram were having an altercation. Arthur moved away from the voices towards the front door. Then he clearly heard Abigail say, "Hiram, I am going to ask him whether you like it or not."

Rutland's Blues and Greys

The large doors of the sitting room opened and Abigail appeared, a handkerchief held to her face. Hiram was close behind. "But my dear…" He stopped when he saw Arthur. Abigail lifted her tear-stained face and also saw him. "Oh, Arthur, please will you come into the drawing room for a moment," she said.

Arthur nodded and then followed her and Hiram back into the room. Abigail sat down on a settee, gestured to the settee opposite and said, "Please sit down."

Arthur sat facing her and Hiram, who had seated himself beside his wife. "Arthur, I have a big favour to ask of you. Hiram says I shouldn't, but it is so important to me, I'm going to anyway."

"If there is anything I can do within my power, Abigail, you know I'll willingly help you."

She dabbed her eyes and said, "You know that I have a brother fighting with the Southern Army. He's in the cavalry and was taken prisoner at South Mountain in September." Arthur nodded his remembrance of the date. That was the battle which preceded Antietam.

"I learned two weeks ago that he's being held in a prison close to Washington." She paused. "He is in Fort Delaware, in the middle of the Delaware River." She bowed her head and cried quietly into her hands.

Hiram continued, "We've tried to see him or even contact him but with no success." He looked at Abigail and then said, "We understand that the prison is badly run and the prisoners are suffering."

Abigail lifted her tear-streaked face. "Oh, Arthur, would you please try and see him? You're our only hope. I must know how he is and let him know that we'll do all we can for him."

Arthur nodded. "Of course I will. I might not be successful but I'd be very surprised if I was refused admission."

Hiram put his arm around Abigail, who was now sobbing. "Thank you, Arthur," he said.

Arthur stood up. "I'll take my leave now but, firstly, thank you so much for your hospitality."

Abigail stood up and looked at him with tear-filled eyes. "Goodbye, Arthur. Thank you for coming. It was so lovely having you here." He stepped forward and put his arms around her shoulders, then gently hugged her to his chest.

"Abigail, rest assured I'll do all that I possibly can to find your brother." He kissed her hair and turned to shake Hiram's hand. In silence he walked out of the room and into the hall.

It took a week before Arthur was able to confirm to Abigail that her brother was indeed incarcerated inside Fort Delaware with other prisoners of war. She sent a packet of chocolate and coffee beans for Jonathan if Arthur was able to meet him.

Chapter 12

Early in the morning of January 30th 1863 Arthur stood by the River Delaware, on the quayside at Delaware City. He was waiting for the supply ferry to come downstream to pick him up and take him across the river to the Union prison on Pea Patch Island. Through the early morning gloom he could just make out the loom of the island in the centre of the river, lying low on the near horizon. Faintly visible on the southern tip was the bulk of Fort Delaware, the prison where he was told numerous Confederate soldiers were being held as prisoners of war.

By the time the ferry had taken him across the swiftly running water and he had disembarked, he was feeling the bitter cold right through his heavy uniform, even though he was wearing his dark-blue artillery caped overcoat.

He walked from the landing stage and up the long slope towards the heavy double gates of the Fort. He crossed on the drawbridge over the moat to the sally port entrance sct in the outer wall where a soldier stood with a rifle on his shoulder.

"I wish to see Captain La Trobe." The soldier did not salute or comment, he just pointed towards the small door in the outer wall.

Arthur pushed it open and entered the outer yard which was obviously a parade ground. In the corner just beyond the sally port he could see a partially open door; he walked over to it and pulled it fully open. Inside were a couple of soldiers, each with a blanket around his shoulders, huddled round a stove in the corner of the small room. As he entered and closed the door behind him, they both looked up but made no comment.

"I wish to see Captain La Trobe," he said.

"Is he a prisoner here?" asked one of the men.

"Yes, he is."

"Well, you'll have to wait."

"Wait for what?" asked Arthur.

"Until I'm ready to take you there," the soldier replied with a smirk to his companion.

"Then you will take me right now," instructed Arthur. "If you don't, I will report you to the Governor for being obstructive."

"For being what?"

"Obstructive. Do you know what that is?" asked Arthur.

"Nope," was the reply, but this did not lead to any action from either of the privates, both of whom remained huddled round the stove.

"You'll find out shortly," said Arthur. He opened the door again and walked out onto the parade ground, ensuring that the door remained fully open. He walked across the square towards another pair of gates set in the walls of the large building opposite.

"Hey. Where the hell d'you think you're goin'," shouted a voice behind him, presumably one of the men from the small office. Arthur ignored the call and strode towards the gates. He heard the sound of a man running behind him and then felt a hand pull at his sleeve. Arthur turned instantly and in a loud authoritarian voice said, "Don't you dare touch me! You're a disgrace of a soldier."

"Who the hell are you?" asked the soldier.

"I am Colonel Rutland of Her Majesty's Royal Artillery on official business to see Captain La Trobe."

The soldier looked amazed, and then scared. "Sorry, Colonel. Why didn't you say that in the beginning."

Arthur ignored the stupid remark and said, "Take me to the Captain at once."

The man pointed towards the main building and said, "He's in there but I don't exactly know where."

"Then take me to someone who does." The soldier turned and started walking towards the prison building.

"Is he kin folk to you?"

Arthur ignored the question. The soldier, annoyed by the lack of reply, repeated in a slightly bolder voice, "I said, is he kin folk?"

"That has nothing to do with you whatsoever," said Arthur.

"Now look you've riled me enough," exclaimed the soldier.

"Colonel," said Arthur.

"What?" asked the private.

"'Now look you've riled me enough, Colonel', is what you should have said. Now go on," explained Arthur. The soldier was befuddled by the comment, but by now the two men had reached the double doors.

"Open the door for me, Private," ordered Arthur. By this time the soldier had given in. He knew when he was beaten, so he pulled open the small portal door set in the main double entrance gates. Arthur ducked his head as he entered.

Once inside, the first thing that struck Arthur was the appalling smell of urine and the sight of so much general filth.

A soldier limped towards Arthur. On his faded blue jacket he wore the two tapes of a Corporal. "Can I help you, sir?"

"I wish to see a prisoner. Can you help me?"

"Not directly, sir, but the sergeant may." He pointed towards an open office door through which a sergeant could be seen sitting at a desk reading a newspaper. Arthur entered. The sergeant looked up but did not stand up or speak.

"I wish to see Captain La Trobe," said Arthur.

"He's dead," replied the sergeant.

Arthur, stunned by the statement, asked, "When? How?"

"I dunno. But he's dead."

"How do you know he's dead then?"

"Because I say so. All these traitors should be dead."

"Show me where his living area was."

"Go to hell," said the sergeant and lowered his head to continue reading.

Arthur undid the three buttons of his caped overcoat and opened the front. He then unbuckled the flap of his holster and drew out his Tranter revolver, and pointed the weapon at the sergeant. "You have five seconds to show me where he lived or I'll shoot you in the leg," he said.

The sergeant looked up in shock and instantly stood up with his hands outstretched, "Alright, alright, I'll show you. Just put that goddamn gun away!" Arthur lowered his revolver and replaced the weapon in its holster.

"This way," said the sergeant.

"Colonel."

"What?" said the sergeant.

"This way, Colonel."

"Oh sure, this way, Colonel." It was obvious to Arthur that so far he had only met the bullies of the prison; there was not one man of courage to be seen yet.

The sergeant led the way out of the office, and on seeing the corporal called out, "Hey, Jackass, take this guy to the second floor officers' section. He wants to see La Trobe."

"You said he was dead!" exclaimed Arthur.

"Oh, well, he might still be alive but not for long." Then he said to the corporal, "Take him away, Jackass, for God's sake," and went back into his office.

The corporal limped over to Arthur and saluted. "You wanted to see Captain La Trobe, sir?"

"Yes, please, corporal."

"If you'll follow me, it's some way and up a number of stairs." He turned and started to limp towards a large stairway.

"Is Jackass your real name?" asked Arthur.

"Hell, no, sir. My name is Henry Jackson but these sons of … sorry, sir, lousy scum call me Jackass because I was wounded at Bull Run where Stonewall Jackson the Rebel General made his stand. None of these layabouts have ever been to war." He stopped walking and turned to face Arthur. "They treat the prisoners awful bad here, sir. If these so-called guards had ever seen battle, they'd understand what it's all about." He started to limp up the stairs very slowly. "I'm sorry for bein' so slow but my leg seizes up after a while."

"Take your time, Jackson. I'm in no hurry" At the top of the stairs they turned right and walked down a long corridor that had bolted doors off it on either side. The stench was getting worse.

Jackson unbolted a door and looked in. "Is Captain La Trobe in here?"

"No, he's in 26."

Jackson came out and bolted the door. They walked down the corridor until they reached a door numbered 26. Again Jackson unbolted the door and opened it. "Is Captain La Trobe in here?"

Arthur heard a mumbled reply, and then Jackson said, "Well, he's got a visitor."

As Jackson stepped back and held open the door, Arthur walked through the opening and into a scene from hell. Ten men were lying or sitting on truckle beds. All of them were dressed in various shades of a grey uniform; some had blankets around their shoulders.

Dirty matted beards covered their mouths and chins. They all turned to look at Arthur and, under the beards and filth, a look of amazement showed on every face. For there in front of their disbelieving eyes was an immaculately turned-out officer, washed and shaved, in a clean, dark-blue, caped overcoat wearing a Field cap with a red band around it and with an unusual badge on the front.

"I'm seeking Captain La Trobe," said Arthur.

No one replied, and then one of the men said "Certainly, sir." He rose and walked to a bed where a man was lying down. Gently, he shook the recumbent figure saying, "Jonathan, someone to see you."

Slowly, the man on the bed lifted himself up onto his elbow, and turned to face Arthur.

Arthur's mouth dropped open; he was appalled at the sight in front of him. La Trobe's face, above the filthy matted beard, was a mass of dried blood and swollen flesh. Gradually, he turned, sat on the edge, and then started to rise from the bed but Arthur came over saying, "No, don't get up." He sat down on the side of the bed and looked at La Trobe closely.

"What happened to you?" he asked.

La Trobe wiped the back of his filthy hand across his mouth. "I guess officially I fell down the stairs." He coughed a deep racking cough.

Arthur turned to face the other officers in the room, who by now were all standing up. "What did happen?" he asked. No reply came, then one man said, "Who are you, sir?"

"Oh, I beg your pardon. I'm Colonel Arthur Rutland of Her Majesty's Royal Artillery. I'm a military attaché for the British Government. I was asked by Captain La Trobe's sister to come and see him." He waved his arm around the room. "But this is appalling."

He looked at the officers and again asked, "What happened to him?"

"Will you be reporting back to the Governor here, sir?" asked an officer.

"No. I report to no one except my senior British officer in Washington. Now, what happened?"

"Jon was beaten up by the main Guard Sergeant because he went to the help of a young officer who was having an epileptic fit. The guards were tormenting the poor man and Jon just couldn't stand it, so he tried to get the man away to the hospital. They just kicked him and beat him up and left both of them."

"Has Jon been to hospital for his wounds?"

"Oh no. They don't take any of us there for 'accidental' wounds like this. We either get better or we die."

Arthur turned to Jon. "Abigail asked me to come and see you. She asked me to bring something for you." Arthur felt inside his caped overcoat and brought out the packet. "Here is some chocolate, and some coffee beans."

Jon looked in silence at the packet and then gently put his hand on it. "Thank you, sir. Please give it to Jimmy." He waved his hand towards the other officers. Arthur turned and an officer came forward.

Arthur held out the packet to be taken when the door of the cell burst open. In strode a Union Army Captain followed by the sergeant from the office below.

"There he is, sir," said the sergeant.

Rutland's Blues and Greys

"Who are you and what are you doing here?" asked the Captain. Arthur did not stand; he remained sitting on the bed beside Jon.

"I am Colonel Rutland here to visit Captain La Trobe."

"Well, you can't. Get out now," he said and put out his hand towards the officer holding Arthur's parcel. "I'll take that. Now get out."

Arthur stood up and in a sharp stentorian voice said, "Captain!" The Captain turned with a look of surprise on his face. "I am a senior officer in Her Majesty's Army on secondment to the Army of the Potomac. You will address me as Colonel or sir."

"Well, sir," said the Captain with a sneer. "I'm telling you to get out – now."

"I will leave when I have finished my visit here with Captain La Trobe."

"Will you hell!" exclaimed the Captain.

"I'm here with the permission and authority of General Burnside. Do you wish me to pass on your insubordinate comment when I see him?"

"You can stay here for five minutes. That's all that's officially allowed."

"What's your name, Captain?" asked Arthur.

"I'm Captain Hawkes in charge of the security of this prison. Now is there anything else Colonel?" he sneered.

"Yes, and listen very carefully," replied Arthur. He opened his caped overcoat, pulled it off his shoulders and lowered the garment onto the bed. He now stood in the full panoply of his uniform, from his red-banded staff cap down to the broad red stripes on his trouser legs and his spurred boots, showing medals and rank, together with his holstered revolver and sword. He had everyone's attention in the filthy cell.

"Have you heard of General Hooker? 'Fighting Joe' Hooker?" he asked.

"Yes," replied Hawkes with a frown on his face.

"When I return to First Army Corps, I will speak to General Hooker and tell him that at Fort Delaware there is a detachment of Federal infantry who are fit, well fed and uniformed but are poorly trained. I will suggest to General Hooker that they are exchanged for a detachment of wounded veterans who can no longer fight. You, Captain, and your despicable sergeant, can then be trained to act as proper soldiers. Are you still listening carefully, Captain?"

Hawkes' face had frozen. "Yes."

"Yes what?" barked Arthur.

"Yes, sir."

"This prison is a disgrace to a civilised nation. You and the guards are just bullying savages. You will change at once. I'll return here in two weeks' time. If things are not a great deal better, then you will all be transferred to the fighting, that I promise you."

"Colonel, I can't do anything without the Governor's permission."

"Nonsense! I'll see the Governor regarding food and bedding, but you can stop this bullying at once. And I mean at once, do you fully understand?"

"Yes, sir."

From the small group of Southern officers standing at the end of the cell, came a voice. "Gee whillikins, that's tellin' 'em."

Arthur snapped his head round to look behind him at the group of huddled Confederate officers. "Silence!" he ordered. "You are not a party to this conversation."

Everyone froze. Union and Confederate officers alike were suddenly in awe of this tall, impressive British officer whose strong character and fearsome personality filled every part of the filthy cell. Everyone there inside it knew that here was a senior officer who was not to be crossed; his barely controlled, pent-up fury was almost a physical presence.

He turned back to face Hawkes, and in a hard, even biting tone said, "After I have finished my visit here with Captain La Trobe, I want Corporal Jackson available to take me to the hospital area and then to the Governor's office. You will inform the Governor that I would like to see him in about one hour's time."

Captain Hawkes was stunned. He knew that his current comfortable little world had been hit by a whirlwind but he was not sure what he could retain. He decided to leave, and think about it after talking to the Governor.

"Is that all clear, Captain?" asked Arthur with an edge to his voice.

"Yes, sir."

"Then you are dismissed." The Captain saluted and, pushing the sergeant ahead of him, left the cell.

Arthur faced the silent and huddled prisoners. "All I've said is true and I'll do all in my power to improve your situation here." He sat down again on the bed and looked closely at Jonathan. The face was filthy and bloody but Arthur could just see a slight smile in his eyes. He put his hand on Jon's and said, "I'm going to get the surgeon to see you as soon as possible." Jonathan nodded his head. He tried to speak but nothing came. Then a tear slid down his bloody and filthy face and landed on Arthur's hand.

Arthur stood and picked up his coat. "Gentlemen, I'm sorry I can't do more for you now, but I will shortly."

A Southern officer stepped forward and saluted. "Colonel, I'm Major Mark Stevenson. What you have just done will give hope to all the men inside this prison. I can't…. I…" He stopped and looked down at the floor, unable to continue.

Arthur bowed his head and nodded. He could feel the deep emotion in those few words. These men were going through a mental and physical hell without any sight of what the future would be, other than utter despair.

He swung his caped overcoat back around his shoulders. "I hope that things'll be better, but I recommend that you do not allow any of your men to be overenthusiastic. I'm sure the guards can cause great trouble for you and still be inside their rules." He started to leave the cell, then turned round and asked, "Can you buy food and bedding with Northern dollars?"

"Yes sir, we surely can," replied the Major. "There's a sutler that turns up once a week."

Arthur walked back to the first bed and turned out his pockets of coins and added some notes to let them fall on the bare mattress. He left the cell with the Confederate prisoners almost in a state of shock.

Outside in the corridor stood Jackson. "Shoot, Colonel. You surely told 'em."

Rutland's Blues and Greys

Arthur put his finger to his mouth to denote that Jackson should be silent.

"Will you take me to the Prison Hospital now, please?"

"Yes, sir, certainly, sir" replied the Corporal with enthusiasm. "Just follow me, Colonel." And he limped off down the corridor.

Chapter 13

Following Jackson was slow, but eventually they reached a wide corridor on the ground floor with a door marked 'Sick Room'. Jackson opened the door and stood back for Arthur to enter. It was a large room with twenty beds, complete with blankets, all well spaced apart. Just inside the room was a small office with a desk at which a man in uniform was standing.

"Can I help you?" he asked.

"I am Colonel Rutland, military attaché to the British Embassy in Washington."

The young officer did not move. He appeared to be in stunned amazement and then he said. "And I, sir, am Lieutenant Walker, supposedly the doctor of this terrible place."

This time it was Arthur who was amazed at the comment. "Supposedly the doctor?" he queried.

"Colonel," said Walker. "Look at this ward. All these clean beds are ready for use. I've reasonable amounts of medicine and dressings but no patients. Why? Because I'm not allowed to go into the prison. I'm

Rutland's Blues and Greys

only allowed to treat prisoners who're brought into here. By which time they're either nearly dead or are dying. This prison's an awful place." He looked down at the floor and continued. "I should do more and complain harder but I'm a coward at heart."

"I think you might be too hard on yourself, Lieutenant. You're outranked by Captain Hawkes, who I'm presume wouldn't let you help the prisoners."

"That's right, Colonel, but I could have pushed harder with the Governor but.."

"But what, Lieutenant?" asked Arthur.

"The Governor is not a very strong-minded man and he leaves the responsibility of security and the general running of the prison to Captain Hawkes. So a complaint to the Governor ends up with Captain."

"Who actually is the Governor?"

"He's called Colonel Burdett, but he's not real Army. He's a wealthy political appointee who revels in the glory of being a senior officer, sir." Walker stopped. "I've said too much."

Arthur looked around at the small but clean hospital area.

"I'm going to see Colonel Burdett now," he said, "and I shall warn him that the responsibility of the prison is firmly his and that I'm about to give a very bad report because of the way it is run by Captain Hawkes." As he spoke, he slowly walked down the line of beds, then stopped and, looking at Walker, said, "I want you to go to cell 26 and look at Captain La Trobe. He's been attacked by the guards and is in a bad way. Whether he needs just medical dressing or actual hospital care, I don't know."

Arthur could see Walker gently shaking his head. "Colonel, I can't go in there without the Captain's permission. The guards'll stop me"

Arthur put his hand on the Lieutenant's arm. "Now is the chance to show your strength. I am ordering you to go and tend the needs of Captain La Trobe and any other officer in cell 26. I'm a Colonel, which outranks a mere Captain, and I'm on the staff of General Burnside."

Arthur walked back towards the entrance of the ward. "I don't think you'll have any trouble for the next hour or so because I'm going to see the Governor and I'm sure that Hawkes will be there ahead of me."

"I'll go straight away, Colonel," said Walker. "And I'll bring La Trobe back here for an examination. I expect the very least he could do with is a decent bed for a night or two."

"Thank you. I'll call in again when I return in about two week's time."

Jackson was waiting patiently outside in the corridor. "Where to now, Colonel?" he asked.

"The Governor's office. But before we go, how many of the guards are like you, reasonably understanding, and how many like Captain Hawkes and the Sergeant?" Jackson leaned against the wall, pushed his cap back and scratched his head.

"Well, Colonel, that's not an easy one to answer, but most of the old veterans who've fought against the reb's feel easy-going with this lot. While most of the nasties ain't never seen a rebel fightin', let alone heard a gun bein' fired," he paused again. "I guess it's about half and half but the mean ones are the ones with the extra stripes or bits on their shoulders."

Rutland's Blues and Greys

"Among the veterans are there any sergeants or educated men?"

"Well Colonel, the good sergeants are now privates and the only officer other than Captain Hawkes is a youngster who does exactly what the Captain says. But there is Billy Maylam; he's a good man and was a teacher before the war."

"Do you know where he is now?"

"Yup, he's in the bunkhouse."

"Will you take me there, please, Corporal?"

"This way, Colonel," said Jackson and set off down the corridor.

The guards' bunkhouses were a series of small dormitories holding six men. Each room was set off the small mess area, in the centre of which there was one large table.

Jackson looked into his bunkhouse where Maylam was sitting on a bed reading a book. He was wearing army trousers with the braces over his long sleeved vest. Jackson spoke to him while Arthur waited outside.

Maylam quickly put on his jacket and belt, then grabbed his cap and came out to the mess table. He saluted. "You wanted to see me, sir?"

As Maylam saluted, Arthur noticed that most of the fingers were missing from his right hand. It seemed he only had a thumb and a forefinger left.

Arthur returned the salute and said, "When were you wounded?"

"In May '62 at Williamsburg. I was hit in the hand and the hip by a couple of Minie bullets. They sure slowed me down, sir."

Arthur smiled at the casualness. He also noticed that Maylam's faded uniform showed where there had once been sergeant's stripes.

"Were you just an infantryman?"

"No, sir." Maylam stood a little more upright and almost puffed out his chest. "I was a Quartermaster Sergeant in charge of all company stores, sir."

"Why are you here as a private?"

Maylam shrugged his shoulders. "After I came out of hospital, I was told I was unfit to fight, and my old company had been wiped out. But I wasn't bad enough to be discharged. So I was sent here to this terrible place, and Captain Hawkes busted me."

"But surely you had a substantive rank?"

"A what, sir?" asked Maylam with a frown.

"I assume your rank as Quartermaster Sergeant was not a temporary rank but permanent. Is that right?"

"Yup, that's right, sir, but that don't mean much to Captain Hawkes. If he don't like you, you get busted."

Arthur reached inside his coat to his jacket pocket and pulled out his gunner's notepad. He handed it to Maylam and said, "Write your name, number and proper rank in there for me, please."

With a surprised look on his face Maylam took the pad. He went to the mess table, opened the pad and quickly wrote down the information. Arthur looked at it, folded the pad and put it in his pocket.

"Thank you, Maylam," he said and then turned to Jackson. "Now I would like to see the Governor."

Billy Maylam, with a surprised look on his face, saluted as Arthur left the mess area.

On the polished door was a brass plate saying 'Colonel M. Burdett, Governor.' Arthur knocked but he did not wait for a reply and pushed the door open. A clerk seated at a desk looked up and said, "Can I help you?"

"I'm here to see the Governor."

"I'm not sure if he's available," replied the clerk.

"He will be," said Arthur. "Go and tell him that Colonel Rutland is here to see him at once."

"But.." started the clerk.

"Go and tell him now," ordered Arthur. The clerk got up from the desk, opened a door at the far end of the room and went inside.

Arthur decided to give him just thirty seconds and, if he did not reappear by then, he would go into the office. The clerk made it with ten seconds to spare. "The Governor will see you."

Arthur marched into an office that had a large desk situated at the end of the room. A tubby man in his late sixties was seated at it with Captain Hawkes standing at his right elbow.

"Good afternoon, Governor. I am Colonel Rutland visiting Captain La Trobe, as I'm sure you're fully aware."

"Good afternoon, Colonel. How can I help you? I'm afraid I can only spare you a few minutes." He did not make any offer for Arthur to sit.

Arthur took off his cap, pulled open his coat and sat down on the leather wing chair facing the Governor. "I think, Governor, you'll spare as long as it takes for me to make you understand what I want."

"The Governor is not prepared to be spoken to like that," interrupted Captain Hawkes.

"Captain, if you are to be part of this discussion and wish to address me, you will either call me sir or Colonel." Arthur did not wait for any acknowledgment from Hawkes but turned to Burdett.

"As Governor of this prison, you obviously have a great number of serious responsibilities." Burdett puffed himself up at this comment. "Yes, well I do have….."

Arthur cut across him saying "But it appears that there are a number of faults in your system that are highly detrimental to the Federal Military system."

Arthur sat back and crossed his legs to show that he was completely at his ease. "Firstly, against all measures of modern civilised decency, you are allowing the inmates of this prisoner of war camp to suffer unnecessarily."

"That is a lie," cried Captain Hawkes.

Arthur again ignored the man. "Governor, you've been badly let down by your staff, who have failed you miserably in not ensuring a minimum of care for the prisoners."

"Come, come Colonel," said the Burdett wriggling in his chair "I think that is not….."

Again Arthur ignored the interruption and continued. "These junior underlings have endangered you, your career and your good name. For it is you and only you who will take the blame when the disgrace of this prison is exposed."

"And what disgrace is that, Colonel?" asked Hawkes

"I will tell the Governor shortly." Arthur looked intently at Burdett. "Do you know how many prisoners you have here?"

"Err, well not exactly but Captain Hawkes here has all the details."

"Do you know how much food is supplied, how much it costs and how much is claimed for?" As there was no answer, Arthur continued. "Do you ever visit the actual cells to see what state the prisoners are kept in?"

"I expect Captain Hawkes to control all these things. I'm much too busy to chase up all these day-to-day actions," replied Burdett.

Arthur paused. He was about to ask the question that would turn the battle in his favour or ruin his chances of winning it.

"Are you aware that the senior officer in charge of the prison security is assisting prisoners to leave the prison, and benefiting from this action?"

"That is a lie!" shouted Hawkes. Arthur gave Hawkes a blistering look.

"Colonel," murmured Hawkes.

"I trust you can prove this allegation, Colonel?" asked Burdett.

"I can and I will, but not while the accused man is in the room. Wait outside, Captain," ordered Arthur.

The Captain's mouth dropped open and he gasped "But…"

Burdett waved his hand at him. "Wait outside, Captain. I will call you in shortly." Hawkes left the office with a great show of reluctance.

"Now, Colonel," said the Governor. "I hope you can substantiate your extraordinary statement."

"Mr Burdett," said Arthur, showing a disdain for Burdett's military rank. "I'm on the staff of General Burnside, and I also make regular reports to the British Ambassador in Washington. The appalling state of this prison is a disgrace to the Federal Government, and I'll have no reservations in making my adverse reports available to all those I've just mentioned - and the English press. They will undoubtedly inform the Southern Confederate papers and the Northern Federal papers will pick up the whole scandal. Your name will be prominent. You, not your subordinates, will take all the blame."

Burdett was sitting forward, with his arms on his desk, looking decidedly pale if not sick. "But it is not my fault if Hawkes has made these errors of judgement."

"It is your name that will be on the headlines, not his," said Arthur.

Burdett pulled a large handkerchief from his pocket and mopped the perspiration from his glistening brow. Then he leaned forward. "You said that he'd assisted prisoners to escape and taken bribes. With that proof I can make sure he's cashiered and disgraced. Now what information do you have on him?"

"Governor, you didn't listen carefully enough. I said that I had proof that Captain Hawkes had assisted prisoners to leave the prison, and that he had benefited from it personally."

"Yes, yes. How?"

"By withholding food and medicine he has allowed prisoners to die unnecessarily. These unfortunates

Rutland's Blues and Greys

escaped from this hellhole by dying, assisted by Hawkes. His reward is personal hatred and a twisted sense of duty. Any court martial would cashier him and you immediately." Burdett leaned back, the look of terror on his face again.

"You, Governor, are an unwitting accomplice to this crime. Unwitting because you allowed the control of the prison to slip from your hands into the control of this sadist." Arthur watched as these words slowly sank into the Burdett's numbed brain.

"There is only one way that you can escape from the terror of a public enquiry," continued Arthur.

Burdett leaned forward, an eager look on his face. "Yes, how do I do it?"

"You must firstly convince me that you will improve the life of these prisoners up to a reasonable standard. You will firmly control the running of this establishment and ensure that Captain Hawkes is only allowed the task of security, not that of running the prison." The large handkerchief again wiped the gathering sweat from Burdett's brow.

"Mr Burdett," continued Arthur. "You are no more a Colonel than I am President of the United States, but you can use your rank as it should be used. At present, if a regular senior officer or a prominent politician saw the situation here, you would be rightfully charged and imprisoned. If on the other hand you make firm improvements now and control Hawkes, you might well be criticised but you can at least say you did your best."

Burdett nodded and pulled some sheets of paper towards him. He was ready to take notes. He could see a doomsday approaching that he must answer at, and maybe he was to be told how to avoid the potential trouble.

Arthur continued. "With Hawkes acting as security only, you must absolutely forbid him to have any control of food, clothing, bedding or accommodation. When I have left, I recommend that you tell him of his new position very firmly, and then tell him to wait in his quarters until you call for him.

"Your Medical Officer, Lieutenant Walker is a good man, who also knows what horrors are being committed here. You must go with him to every one of the cells and inspect all parts of this prison from the lavatories upwards. Ask him for his recommendations. You will be horrified at the terrible state that these men are living in.

"I recommend that you reinstate the rank of Private William Maylam. His rank as Quartermaster Sergeant was illegally taken from him by Hawkes. Maylam should be in control of, and account for, all food and clothing coming in. Nothing will be illegally taken, so in future you will not be in trouble."

Burdett scribbled notes as fast as Arthur made each point. Finally he stopped, laid down his pencil and stood up. He turned away from the desk to look out of the slit window at the windswept salt marsh surrounding the fort site. After a minute he faced Arthur again.

"I'll inspect the whole area with Walker and if the situation is as bad as you say, then I'll take all of your advice in total."

Arthur stood up. "Thank you, Governor. I wish to see Walker in the hospital again. He'll have Captain La

Rutland's Blues and Greys

Trobe there, who has been badly beaten by your Guard Sergeant. I think that the Captain will live – if he had died, then you'd have had a murder enquiry on your hands. I suggest that you deal with the Guard Sergeant in the strongest possible way." Burdett, still standing, nodded his bowed head.

"Shall I instruct Lieutenant Walker to come and see you now?" asked Arthur.

"If you would, Colonel."

"I'll return in two to three weeks' time to see how Captain La Trobe is recovering." Again Burdett nodded, knowing full well that he was also to be inspected at that time.

Arthur turned and without comment, or a salute, left the room.

In the outer office Hawkes stopped his anxious walking back and forth. He watched as Arthur walked across to the outer door and then he heard Burdett call out, "Come in here, Captain."

Outside the Governor's office Arthur said to Jackson, "The last trip, Corporal. Please take me back to the Sick Room."

"Shoot, Colonel, I'd take you to hell and back and wait outside because of all the kerfuffle you're creatin'. By God, this place needed you a long time ago." Arthur smiled and waved his hand. "Lead on, Jackson - not to hell, just the Sick Room."

La Trobe was lying in a bed and appeared to be sleeping. His face had been washed and his beard cut back with scissors. Walker came over to stand by Arthur.

"My God, sir, they'd given him one hell of a kicking," he said. "At least three ribs are broken, but luckily they're all back in place and with care and keeping him still, they'll mend."

"How about his face?" asked Arthur, a deep frown across his brow.

"A broken nose, but the cheek bones are intact." Walker looked at Arthur's anxious face. "Don't worry sir. He'll be fit in a couple of weeks' time. I'll keep him here as long as possible. I've given him a dose of laudanum so he'll sleep for a few hours."

"Thank you," murmured Arthur. He walked up the ward towards the office area, and then he said, "Your time has come, Lieutenant."

Walker frowned. "My time, sir?"

"I've made the Governor agree that Hawkes is to be security only and I've arranged for a new Quartermaster Sergeant to be in charge of stores. But mainly, the Governor has agreed that he'll inspect the whole of the prison – along with you. You're to take notes and tell him of all that is wanted and the work that must be done.

"I suggest you give the prisoners brushes and buckets so that they can clean up their own cells. Be firm. I think he'll agree to any reasonable request. Your main trouble will be putting pressure on the authorities to give you the food and equipment needed, but it's up to you. He wants to see you now"

As Arthur spoke, a smile broke out on Walker's face. "Yes, sir! I'll get it done."

"I'll come back to see La Trobe in a few weeks, time," said Arthur. "I hope you'll have some good news for me." He shrugged his cape into position and then added, "When you make your inspection, ask Corporal Jackson if you've seen everything. He knows this prison much better than either the Governor or you. Also will you have a look at Jackson's leg? I think he should be on light duties, not walking all over the prison."

Ten minutes later Arthur was back at the jetty watching the supply ferry approach. He felt that it had been a good day's work but now he was hungry and tired. He mainly wanted a stiff whisky to take away the stench of this hellhole.

As he had to return direct to Washington, he could not visit the Eaves so he would have to write to Abigail – it would be a difficult letter. Jonathan was in a bad way but at least he was alive. Arthur wondered if Sir Percy Wyndham just might be able to pull a few strings and get him paroled. And of course he had to write to Millie – it would be an extra long letter this time.

Chapter 14

It was five weeks later that Arthur was able to get away from Washington and arrange a visit to see the Eaves again before he went on to Fort Delaware.

Though he had written to Hiram and Abigail a few days beforehand, and they had said they would be pleased to have him stay, he was surprised to find that neither of them was at home when he arrived. A butler showed him to the sitting room and gave him a whisky with the news that the Eaves should be back in an hour or so.

In fact it was only half an hour before the sitting room doors were flung wide open and Abigail entered with a flourish and a beautiful warm welcoming smile.

"Oh, Arthur, it is so good to see you." She gave him a hug and a kiss on his cheek before he could say anything. "I am so sorry we kept you waiting," she continued. "But I've been so busy."

Behind her Hiram stood with a wry smile on his face and said, "You don't know what you've started, Arthur."

"I'm at a complete loss other than it is marvellous to see you both in such high spirits."

Abigail sat down on the large settee. "You are going to see Jonathan again?" she asked, looking eagerly at Arthur. "And have you any news?"

Arthur also sat down opposite Abigail and leaned forward. "Yes, I have got some news, Abigail, but it is not definite or confirmed."

"He will definitely be paroled?" she eagerly asked.

"No," said Arthur. Abigail visibly showed her great disappointment.

"But…" she started.

"Abigail," Arthur interrupted her. "I have not got anything definite - but he is being considered for parole, and though far from confirmed, I must say that I have high hopes."

Abigail's beautiful smile flowed across her face again. "I knew you would succeed," she said.

"Abi!" Hiram exploded. "Don't exaggerate. Arthur is being very cautious but hopeful – that does not mean Jon will definitely be paroled." Hiram looked at Arthur. "Am I correct?"

Arthur nodded. But Abigail's optimism was not to be defeated. She smiled at Arthur. "I know you will succeed." Hiram threw his hands in the air in despair.

"Now, Arthur," said Abigail. "Let me tell you what has happened here while you have been in Washington."

"All hell has been let loose," interrupted Hiram.

"Hiram, please control your language." Abigail scowled at her husband. She faced Arthur and said, "After your visit to Jon, and your letter to me, I decided to do something to help other Southern prisoners who are held around here." Arthur felt a deep sensation of worry at this comment but Abigail sailed on with her explanation.

"There is a war prison at Fort McHenry near the harbour here in Baltimore. I decided to visit there and see what the conditions were like." She turned and gave Hiram a dig with her hand. "You were against it at first, but you agree now, don't you?"

Hiram nodded. "Yes, you were right."

"I went with Hiram to the prison and spoke to the Governor. He let us in and said that an officer would show us around. To my surprise, though the conditions are very sordid, they are not like Jon's prison, are they, Hiram?"

Before Hiram could reply, Abigail continued, saying, "We have tried to get in extra food and money for food, but the Governor said that was not acceptable. The authorities should look after all their needs."

"Abi pushed a little too far in trying to get extra food in," said Hiram. "But with the fact that we are visiting the prison occasionally, I don't think things will get any worse."

"How did the Governor feel about all of this, knowing that Abigail was from the South?" asked Arthur.

"Oh, Abi had a scheme to counter that," smiled Hiram

"A scheme?" queried Arthur.

"Oh for sure, Arthur," said Abigail. "I am a scheming little hussy." She sat forward on the edge of the sofa. "There are Union wounded soldiers in the National Hotel Hospital on Camden Street, so I decided that I

Rutland's Blues and Greys

would visit there regularly to write letters and give what help I could. I thought that was a very clever counter to prove I was not a Confederate supporter." She paused. "In fact it made me rather ashamed. After I had made a couple of calls, I realised that those poor boys with terrible wounds or missing an arm are just the same as the boys from home in the South. I now visit the National frequently because I want to help them." She hung her head in sadness and whispered. "And they do so need help."

Hiram looked down at his wife, while Arthur gave a gentle nod. "My goodness, Hiram," he said. "You have an amazing personality in Abigail. I don't think she lets much stand in her way when she makes up her mind."

Arthur climbed off the supply ferry that had taken him across the bitterly cold Delaware River to Pea Patch Island and the forbidding Fort Delaware.

As he crossed the drawbridge again, he saw the sentry who was posted just outside the sally port gate bring his musket to the high port and call out, "Halt and state your name."

Arthur stopped and replied, "I am Colonel Rutland to see the Governor."

With his fist the sentry banged the sally port door behind him. It opened and a Corporal appeared.

"Who are you?" he asked.

"I am Colonel Rutland to see the Governor."

"Will you come through here, sir?" said the Corporal and stepped back through the sally port door. Arthur followed him towards the small office. The Corporal looked at a list lying on the office table. "Yes, Colonel. He is expecting you."

He called a second sentry over. "Take the Colonel to the Governor's office." The soldier saluted Arthur and said, "This way, sir."

Arthur followed the man across the parade ground and into the main building. He immediately noticed that the air was fresher and there was no longer the stench of urine. He also saw that, though it was very cold, there were a number of Confederate soldiers walking around outside. They were also moving freely inside the buildings.

Eventually having climbed up a flight of stairs, the Federal soldier led him to the Governor's door. Arthur knocked and entered. A clerk got up from his desk and said, "Can I help you sir?"

"Colonel Rutland to see the Governor."

"Oh, yes, sir. Please wait a moment." The clerk knocked at the inner office door and went in. He reappeared instantly "Will you come in, sir?"

Arthur walked into the office to see Governor Burdett standing in the middle of the room with his hand outstretched.

"Welcome, Colonel. It's very good to see you."

Arthur shook his hand and said, "Thank you."

Burdett waved his hand at the large leather chair and said, "Please sit down, sir. Can I take your coat?"

Arthur shook his head, "No, thank you. I want to see Captain La Trobe if I may, and then return with the supply ferry."

"Of course." Burdett sat behind the desk. "I hope you can see that a great deal has changed. I think most of your advice has been taken plus some extras. Hawkes is only in charge of security. I had the sergeant demoted and posted to a fighting regiment. I was going to do the same with Hawkes, but I decided that he'd be completely controlled by his knowing that he could also be moved at a moment's notice."

Burdett stood up and sat on the edge of his desk. "As you will see when you go around, the prisoners are in far better conditions and the Medical Officer is in a much more powerful position. You will also find that Quartermaster Sergeant Maylam has improved supplies considerably." He stood up and walked over to the fireplace and looked at the burning logs. "However, I'm in a difficult position. Despite my frequent requests, and Maylam's continued chasing, we are still well short of the rations needed to feed all the prisoners properly. Also, there have been one hundred and fifty seven extra prisoners since Antietam."

He turned to face Arthur. "You must understand, Colonel, that there's no use in trying to get help or supplies from the surrounding areas. There are too many local men who are away fighting with the Union Army. No one'll give any assistance to these imprisoned rebels while their brothers, husbands or sons are being killed by other rebels."

He walked round his desk again and sat down. "Colonel, I'm ashamed of my slack attitude to these men before your first visit and I'm now fully aware of what I must do to keep them, to the best of my ability, in reasonable conditions. But I am finding that the authorities are getting harder and harder. This is all beyond my control."

Arthur remained silent through all of this explanation. Burdett had obviously changed and was doing all that he could. It might be not have been enough but ...

"Governor." Arthur showed respect for Burdett by using this title. "I have never been in a position like you are here, so I don't feel I can make any useful comment. You obviously have a hard task but are tackling it. My compliments."

Arthur stood up. "I would like to see Captain La Trobe now if possible."

"Certainly," replied Burdett. He also stood up and offered his hand, which Arthur shook.

"Colonel," continued Burdett. "I'm in your debt for what you have done. I'll never forget the English officer who descended on us like a whirlwind. We all benefited, prisoners and staff, from your anger. I'm grateful."

Arthur smiled, "Thank you, Governor." He drew himself to attention and gave a formal salute that Burdett acknowledged with a nod of his head. Arthur turned and walked out of the office.

In the outer office the clerk got up form his desk again and said, "Do you wish to see Captain La Trobe, sir?"

Arthur was surprised by the question. "Yes, I do."

"Captain Hawkes has asked him to be in the Guards Mess room, where you can see him privately."

"Thank you."

"The Guard Corporal is outside. He'll show you where the Mess room is, sir."

Arthur opened the door to the corridor. The Guard Corporal, who was waiting outside, saluted and said, "The Guards Mess room, sir?"

"Yes, please."

The two men strode along the corridor and through the prison until they reached the small mess room where Arthur had first met Billy Maylam. As he entered the room, he saw Jonathan, wearing a heavy grey overcoat and his yellow-topped cavalry kepi, seated at a bench. Jonathan got up, saluted Arthur and said. "Good morning, Colonel."

Arthur strode towards him with his hand outstretched. "No, Jonathan. Please call me Arthur." The two men shook hands with the firmness of a strong though short friendship. Arthur gestured for them to sit down opposite to each other on the benches at the table.

"You certainly look a lot better than when I last saw you. How are your ribs?"

"Fine now. Young Lieutenant Walker the MO did a great job. He's been a wonder since he got the power to clean up this prison," said Jonathan. "He'll be pleased to see you."

"I don't think I'll have time, but will you just tell him from me that I was certain he was never a coward."

"Walker a coward!" exclaimed La Trobe.

"He'll understand. So how are things here now?"

"Before you came, Burdett's name was dirt but now he's doing all he can to make our lives as reasonable as possible. Food and supplies are very short but that's the Union Army, not Burdett. Even the guards are short of food. But at least Hawkes is under control. In fact he's a very efficient officer for guard and prisoner discipline. That murderous Sergeant Arnes was busted by Burdett and sent off with everyone jeering. He was the worst."

Jonathan took off his cavalry cap. " Walker got the implements so that we could all clean up the prison and ourselves. So now we sit here and wait for the end of the war." He looked at Arthur. "But tell me about you. How do you know Abigail?"

"I met her and Hiram when I was on board ship coming over last August. We got on so well that I've stayed in touch. Then in January she told me of you being here and asked me to visit."

"Thank God you did. A number of us would have died this winter but for you." He leaned on the table. "But, Arthur, I must know about you in England. Where do you live?"

"I live in an old farmhouse in east Surrey close to the Kent border in South-East England. I'm married and have two children, a boy and a girl. They are twins actually."

"And you left them to come out here?"

"Yes. It sounds strange, but I'm a professional soldier and I get posted all over the world. Sometimes Millie comes with me but mainly she remains at home."

"Millie, is that your wife?"

"Yes, her name is Amelia, but we all call her Millie."

"There's a coincidence. My wife is Amelia, but we call her Amy."

"Do you have children, Jonathan?"

"Yes, two boys. Twelve and fourteen. They're helping to run the plantation."

"What do you grow?"

"Mainly cotton and some rice."

Rutland's Blues and Greys

Arthur paused. He had a question that he had to ask but he was worried about the consequences. "Do you have any slaves?"

"Yes, we have seventeen," said Jonathan. "You are shocked?"

"I suppose I am. I can't understand the basis of owning a human being as a slave."

"Since you have been over here, Arthur, are there a number of things that have surprised you?"

"Yes, many."

"And my workers are one of those?"

Arthur nodded in reply.

"I must have cheap labour to run the plantation," said Jonathan. "I have fourteen men who are my field hands and three women who are servants in the house. All of them and their families are well cared for and fed. I'd never sell them and I'd never beat them. They call out 'good morning' to me each day and I think they're happy

"But they aren't free. They can't just leave," said Arthur

"Do you employ workers on your farm, Arthur?"

"Yes, for all the various jobs."

"But I expect they're paid very low wages."

Arthur nodded.

"Do you give them living quarters for life? And if any of their family are ill, do you care for them?" asked Jonathan

"No, not really," replied Arthur.

"All my negros are fed, sheltered, clothed and cared for from the day they arrive to the day they die."

"But they aren't free to move about, go to another farm – better themselves."

"Can your farm workers always get work when their last job finishes? Do they have to beg for help occasionally?"

"I understand what you are saying; it's just that I can't…."

"It's been happening for many years down South. Without it, our whole cotton production system would fail."

"Are you completely at ease with slavery?" asked Arthur.

Jonathan looked down at his hands. "No, I'm not." There was a silence for a few seconds and then quietly but firmly he said, "But I ain't having any damn Yankee telling me what to do."

"So there's no other way; the South and the North will just have to battle this out with blood?"

Jonathan nodded.

"I was at Antietam," said Arthur. "And at Fredericksburg. It was terrible. There was so much human blood flowing into the soil of those rich cornfields that was all going to waste because there was a difference between two cultures.

Jonathan, still looking at his hands, nodded. "But no Yankee is going to tell me what I can do."

"Do you think the South will win this war?"

"Don't ask me that, Arthur. Please don't ask me."

Arthur felt inside his uniform and pulled out his watch from his fob pocket. "I can't stay much longer, but I have some good news for you."

Jonathan looked up. "Good news?"

Rutland's Blues and Greys

"I've applied for you to be paroled and exchanged. I think there's a very good chance as I did it through the British Embassy and with the support of Colonel Sir Percy Wyndham. Have you heard of him?"

Jonathan smiled. "I sure have. And he's helping me be exchanged?"

Arthur nodded.

"Well, I'll be danged," said Jonathan. "That sure is great news, Arthur. You've no idea how terribly depressing it is to be here. I've been here for so many months but none of us know if it'll be just more months or maybe years." He bowed his head. "I feel so down. I … I'll I never be able to repay you." After a while he murmured, "God damn it, Arthur, that's the second time I've wept in front of you."

"I'm not doing this for you," joked Arthur. "I'm doing this for Abigail. If it wasn't for her, I'd let you rot here." Jonathan looked up at him, smiled and said, "Please will you let me have your home address so I can write you later on?"

Arthur pulled his gunner's notebook out of his pocket and wrote his name and address on a page that he tore out.

"Arthur," said Jonathan. "You've done so much for me but I'm going to ask yet another favour. Could I send a letter for Abigail to this English address for it to be sent to her? I can't send letters direct from the south to the north. They have to go the very long way round through England "

Arthur sat and thought. "I think I should say no, but it should be all right if you only do it a couple of times. The letter must be open so that Millie can read it, and it must not contain anything to do with the military actions."

"I won't let you down, Arthur. I just want to be able to tell Abi that the family and me are well."

Arthur stood up, and Jonathan followed. "If the transfer doesn't go through, then I'll come and visit you again. And, oh, by the way." He felt inside his jacket and brought out an envelope. "Abigail asked me to give this to you. She said it contained money."

Jonathan took the bulky envelope. "Oh my!" he said. "Please tell her 'thank you'. She has no idea what this'll do for the men." Arthur leaned across the table and slapped Jon's arm. "Show me the way out now, please, or I might be taken for an inmate."

Jonathan wiped his hand across his face and smiled. "This way, Colonel."

Outside the door the Guard Corporal stood waiting.

"The Captain and I are going to the sally port now," said Arthur.

"Very good, sir." said the Corporal, "But the parade ground is rather crowded right now, sir." He led the way down the corridor and opened the door onto the parade ground. To Arthur's surprise a large group of prisoners were standing around the door. In front of the crowd was Major Mark Stevenson. Stevenson saluted, then offered his hand and said, "I'm very pleased to see you, Colonel."

Arthur shook his hand. "I'm pleased to see you, Major. You look better than the last time we met."

Stevenson smiled. "A lot better thanks to you, sir. I want to say how appreciative we are of what you have done for us all here."

Arthur nodded and shook the Major's hand again. Jonathan had walked into the crowd and was leading the way towards the main gate. Arthur followed down the avenue created through the group of prisoners. Gradually, they all parted to let him and Jonathan pass, but as they did so they called out "Hi, Colonel" and "Thanks, Colonel." He felt hands pat him on the back and arms, as he walked through them. Jonathan turned his head round and smiled at him. "You sure are a popular person here, Arthur."

At last when Arthur and Jonathan were clear of the cheering crowd and almost across the square, Arthur noticed that the cheering had stopped. Instead it had been replaced by a cry, a howl, a multi-toned yell that swelled up in a cacophony of noise and became all-enveloping as it swamped the square and drowned out all other sounds. Arthur and Jonathan continued towards the sally port with the sound reverberating around them.

"What on earth was that?" exclaimed Arthur.

Jonathan was looking at the ground, gently shaking his head as they walked along, but he had a smile on his face. "I never thought they'd do that for anyone."

"Do what?" asked Arthur.

"You'd only ever hear that sound in battle with our infantry charging," said Jonathan. "That, Arthur, was the 'Rebel Yell'. That's the only Yell I've ever heard when the Rebs weren't going to kill some Yankees."

Roger Carpenter

He turned and took Arthur's hand. "But this one - they did it for you."

Chapter 15

By the time he returned to Washington, Arthur found that there was a confirmation that Jonathan would be definitely be exchanged in the next few days. He quickly sent a telegram to Hiram telling Abigail of the good news.

By now he felt that he had been witness to enough of the bloody battles in this struggle for him to take some time off in preparing and submitting his battle reports. He was told by the British Legation that though he had to submit a copy to the United States authorities, the actual document would be sent to London without any alteration. Having eventually completed it and sent it off, he was surprised that a couple of weeks later there were numerous questions from Horse Guards asking for explanations of his opinion and the facts he had given. These queries all had to be answered in full detail, which took him some considerable time.

Arthur had also decided that after the trauma of Fredericksburg, and the slog of writing up the long and detailed documents, he would do some safer and more convivial work. He decided to do research on the Union artillery by visiting gun and ammunition manufacturers further to the north. An easy but still productive task.

It was during these months of moving up into New York State that he read in the papers of the Union defeat at Chancellorsville, where Hooker was caught off guard by a brilliant encircling movement by Stonewall Jackson, on General Lee's orders.

He also regularly purchased the monthly Harper's magazine, to keep abreast of informed opinion, and he saw, included in the magazine, Sergeant Forrester's articles, complete with his sketches. They were interesting, well presented and accurate to the point of being at times quite shocking in their bluntness to the American reader who had never seen a battle or been made aware of Army life.

On his eventual return to the Legation in Washington, Michael Barrington, Lord Lyons' aide, arranged for Arthur to have the use of a Legation clerk to assist with his report writing. Because of this Arthur would meet Barrington on a regular basis.

One morning as Arthur was checking a copy document written by the clerk, Barrington entered his office and said, "Well, it seems your eccentric Sir Percy is making news then!"

"How's that?" asked Arthur.

"Well, he does rather see this war as bit of an adventure that should be enjoyed like a good game of cricket, and so should be played within gentlemen's rules." Barrington sat down on the chair beside Arthur's desk and folded his newspaper. "Over the past few months he has been plagued by a Confederate Cavalry officer called Mosby, Captain John Singleton Mosby to give him his full name, who seems to have a roving commission to create mayhem anywhere behind Union Lines. But he won't come out and fight face to face with Sir Percy. Sir Percy has called him a horse thief and said he would burn any village that sheltered him."

"That was not a very gentlemanly action," interrupted Arthur.

"I think it was just a wild threat, but strangely it did the trick in bringing Mosby out, though with the wrong results. In March, while you were away up North, Mosby decided to attack Wyndham at his HQ in Fairfax. He tore in, hit hard and tore out again taking a number of prisoners, including a Brigadier who happened to be there at the time. Luckily for Wyndham, he had gone to Washington for a meeting just the day before."

Arthur laughed. "My goodness, I can imagine the explosion when Sir Percy heard that."

Barrington smiled in response. "He was exceedingly angry and swore to have revenge for what he took as a personal insult."

"So how is he making news now?" asked Arthur.

"He has been given a command in General Gregg's division and is currently chasing the Rebels around the Culpeper area. There is talk of some movement of General Lee's army around that part of Virginia."

"Where's Culpeper?" asked Arthur.

"About 60 miles south-west of here, just beyond the Rappahannock river. It's a lovely area just a few miles short of the Blue Ridge mountains."

"You've been there?"

"Yes, in '61 my wife and I rode along the Blue Ridge and down into the breathtakingly beautiful Shenandoah valley but that was before the war started. Now it is the hunting ground of the Confederate army, and one of its best routes for them to follow when marching north. It runs up towards the north-east and is a good line to follow to attack Washington or push into Northern States such as Pennsylvania. To think that lovely area is being ravaged by war. It's terrible."

Barrington stopped and gazed towards the window, obviously lost in the memories of pleasant times past.

Arthur broke the silence. "I think it's about time I went back to the battle area and earned my salt," he said.

"Back to your L Battery ?"

"No. I think I might visit the notorious Sir Percy and have a look at the cavalry guns."

Barrington frowned. "Go with Wyndham and the cavalry?" he queried.

"Yes. I haven't seen any of that type of action and it would be extra interesting."

"Arthur, are you sure? If you go with the cavalry, there is no safe back area. With American cavalry, Union or Confederate, they very much roam and take their base with them."

"I'll make sure I stay away from the front line of action."

"But, Arthur, from what I read and hear, there often is no front line. It's generally all a mix-up."

Arthur appreciated his concern but, as Michael had never seen battle let alone cavalry action, Arthur felt that his own opinion was the best to follow.

Rutland's Blues and Greys

"Don't worry, Michael. I'll keep safe. At the worst I'll just get captured and you'll have to get me swapped with a Rebel."

"If you are certain, Arthur, but please do watch for a quick get-out - to the rear."

Arthur contacted the War Department and found that General Gregg's division, which included Wyndham's command, was based south-west of Washington further along the Orange & Alexandria railroad below Manassas.

He asked for permission to join Sir Percy's force, and within a couple of days he heard that Sir Percy had given his consent for Arthur to be attached to his command. He obtained a military pass and boarded a train in Washington to take him back to the war, which amazingly was only some 50 miles away.

In just a few hours Arthur arrived at Bealeton Station where General Gregg's column was being instructed to leave next morning to sweep round to Brandy Station further down the O&A line where Confederate troops were reported to be around the town of Culpeper.

It was late in the afternoon that Arthur eventually found Wyndham's cavalry lines and made his way past the sentries to reach the joint command HQ.

He reported to the Adjutant in the Regimental Office, who sent a trooper to inform Sir Percy.

While he was waiting, Arthur walked towards the horse line, and he was about to ask if there was any light artillery specifically for the cavalry when he heard his name being called.

"Arthur!" boomed a familiar voice. "Good to see you, old chap." Sure enough, the portly but very active figure of Colonel Wyndham appeared.

"And to see you, Sir Percy," said Arthur putting out his hand, which Percy shook enthusiastically.

"D'you know, when I sent that message saying you could come and visit us, I didn't expect that we would be buzzing off all over the county. But like a hound with a good nose, you found us. Bravo, nothing like a good nose." Sir Percy threw off his coat. "Now, have you got your quarters yet? Hmm? Had some refreshment? What?"

"Atkins, take the Colonel to his digs and then show him where we are messing."

Very early next morning Arthur woke to an unusual trumpet call. He quickly dressed and looked outside his tent. A sergeant walking by said, "That was Officers' mess call, sir. I think we're moving soon so it'd be a good idea to get fed."

"An excellent idea, Sergeant," replied Arthur as he ducked back inside his tent to get his hat and coat.

In the Officers Mess tent, coffee and hard tack was being given out. Arthur put a couple of the hard square biscuits into his pocket. He knew full well the feeling of hunger pangs later on in a day of battle.

A further trumpet call sounded and a Lieutenant said. "That's Regimental Officers to the HQ, sir."

Arthur could see Wyndham surrounded by regimental commanders who were being given their instructions. Arthur stayed well back and waited until he saw that they were all moving off to their various regiments. "Colonel Rutland," called Sir Percy. "Will

Rutland's Blues and Greys

you please accompany Lieutenant Blaker, who is on my staff. He will look after you."

"Thank you, Colonel," called Arthur in reply.

A young cavalry officer stood beside Arthur and said. "Lieutenant Edwin Blaker reporting, sir. We are riding to cross the Rappahannock at Kelly's Ford."

"Is that far away?"

"About an hour's riding, sir."

It was a hour of hard riding that took the command across the river at Kelly's Ford and then on towards the enemy, who were reported to be at Brandy Station close to the O&A rail line. Arthur could hear firing of light artillery and small arms from the north.

"Do you know who that is firing, Lieutenant?"

"We've been told that General Buford is attacking the Rebs from the north so I think it must be him."

The column stopped and Arthur could see Sir Percy at the head looking intently through his glasses at a hill straight ahead. Arthur took out his glasses and saw what was causing the delay. It was a cannon! It looked like a Napoleon and it was set strategically on the hill to defend the approaching road. It would make it deadly for the cavalry to ride directly at - plus there might be more supporting guns out of sight.

"Colonel Wyndham has given orders for skirmishers to be sent out," said Blaker. "He obviously doesn't know what, if any, danger there is ahead."

Arthur saw a messenger gallop to the rear and, within a few minutes, a two-gun section of light artillery galloped up with their guns bouncing behind them. Arthur watched as an artillery Lieutenant brought his section swiftly into action. Everything was done with commendable speed. 'As good as the Royal Horse Artillery,' thought Arthur.

"That's Lt. Clark's section of Martin's Battery, sir."

The two guns immediately started to pound the visible gun and fairly quickly hit it. As there was no replying gunfire, it was assumed that this was the one and only piece.

'But why should there be just one piece, and why was it so obvious?' thought Arthur. 'Unless it was used as a decoy to delay the Union cavalry - but it would only work for a short time - unless it meant that there were support cavalry coming up fast but they needed just a few minutes longer and so it would be worth sacrificing just one artillery piece.'

Sir Percy swung his arm and gave the order for the command to advance. Gradually at first, the regiments swung towards the slope which Blaker said was called Fleetwood Heights. The New Jersey men rode in excellent line to show a steady front straight at the gentle ascent of the hill. Arthur rode well behind and watched. If there was a force of Confederate cavalry or artillery waiting, it should show any moment now.

The New Jersey men trotted on until, just over halfway to the top, a roar of artillery and rifle fire poured from the top of the hill. With an enormous cheer the Union Cavalry charged straight at the Rebel lines with the inevitable result that the Confederate guns could not depress their muzzles quickly enough to keep the charging cavalry in range. The Union men were into the guns and through the line of Greys, who broke and fled. Wyndham's men were in control of the Heights.

Rutland's Blues and Greys

The Northern cavalry with their sabres slashing had ripped through the Greys and right into their rear lines but there waiting was a fresh Rebel Cavalry Regiment; these were the reinforcements that had been on their way while the Union men had been held up by the solitary decoy gun.

Now the Greys charged and threw the Blues back. It was a mad scene of slashing swords and the firing of pistols and carbines. Men and horses were falling and scrambling up to tear through the enemy whichever colour they wore.

The New Jersey men recoiled from the smashing charge of Colonel JEB Stuart's cavalry, the pride of the Confederate Army. Hand to hand, knee to knee the two forces slashed and parried, but the New Jersey men were gradually pushed back.

The two guns of Martin's Battery slammed away into selected targets and helped to slow the Rebel attack, but Arthur thought that the Union Cavalry would be swept from the Heights when the balance of Wyndham's command, the 1st Pennsylvania Regiment and the 1st Maryland, in turn smashed into the side of the Confederate Cavalry. Horses and riders clashed and were bowled over by the force. The chaotic charge and counter charge led to a milling mass of circling stabbing horsemen.

A number of Confederate cavalry, who had managed to deploy unseen on the left flank of Wyndham's command, suddenly attacked in a wild flurry. Arthur could see the Greys starting their charge from the side, when he heard a Union officer order, "Fours, left-about, wheel." The New Jersey line swung to face the new danger. Within only a few seconds they started to move and then they were amongst the Greys, slashing and cutting.

Arthur looked to see where he could leave, but he suddenly remembered Barrington 's comment *'There is no safe back area.'* Barrington was right - he should not be there. This was not an observer's position, this is a pure fighting area - with little use of artillery.

Blaker shouted, "Go to the right, sir. Behind the charge line. You should be safe there."

A group of three Greys had broken away from their cavalry line and were galloping towards the left of the New Jersey men. Blaker drew his sabre and started to yell as he charged towards the group. Arthur watched as he disappeared in a mad, brave charge into the melee.

The fighting was confused – Confederate and Union Cavalry charging from all different directions. Arthur was now fully aware that he had made a terrible mistake in coming, but he could not see a way out of the mess.

His horse gave a sudden squeal, and Arthur felt it try to rear. He pulled the reins hard back and looked round; a bullet had torn a long gash across the horse's rump. He managed to control the hurt animal, and quickly looked around for somewhere he could retire to that had cover. Then he whipped his head round to the right as he heard a terrifying sound. It was a loud, all-swamping Rebel yell - the very sound that had overawed him in Fort Delaware Prison but this time it meant he and the Union Cavalry were the objects of their hate. The howling scream preceded the gut-churning sight of a group of Confederate troopers charging through the light covering of trees. One of them, with his head low along his horse's neck, was riding straight at him with his sword pointed out straight ahead.

Arthur pulled the reins round to get his horse to meet the trooper head on. It was his only chance of avoiding contact and hopefully he could dodge to the side of the trooper at the last second.

He had just turned his mount to face the danger when he felt and heard a thump, then a wet red mist slapped into his face. A bullet had hit his horse's head just below its ears, smashing into its brain and killing it instantly. The bloody mist that was thrown up into his face, blinded Arthur as he felt the animal collapse. It slammed down hard onto its side, trapping Arthur's left leg underneath the corpse. He pushed at the saddle and tugged at his leg but it was hopelessly caught. Then he tried to wriggle over to reach his revolver in its holster, but the charging trooper was almost on him. A sweeping downward sword cut would be the end.

Through the chaos of movement and noise he clearly heard a loud terrible roar of "NO-O-O-O." He twisted his head round and saw that the shout came from another Confederate cavalryman, who looked to be an officer, charging from the left. The officer's hand, without a sword in it, was outstretched, he was shouting at the top of his voice "NO-O-O. STOP!"

The trooper was almost on Arthur when the officer's horse slammed into his horse's side. The trooper just managed to keep his seat but his charge was deflected. The shouting Southern officer roared at the trooper. "Leave him! He's mine!"

'I'm going to be captured,' thought Arthur as the officer turned towards him. Then Arthur saw the blond hair below the cavalry kepi and recognised that it was Jonathan. Jonathan La Trobe!

Arthur tugged again at his trapped leg and felt it coming free as Jonathan rode over to Arthur and looked down at him. "You fool, Arthur. Get out of here now!" he said.

Arthur pulled his leg clear and struggled to his feet.

Jon pointed over to his left. "Go that way! Get out now!" He spun his horse round and yelled over his shoulder as he galloped away. "For God's sake, go home. Go back to Millie."

Over to the left Arthur could see the light guns still being used, but they now did not seem to be having a great deal of effect. He scrambled through the undergrowth and ran towards them and eventually reached the gun site which was a mass of swirling gun horses.

The Union cavalry were charging up the hill yet again and Arthur could see Wyndham well in front waving his sword. The crowd of fighting men was all mixed up but then he could see that gradually the Union cavalry was again being pushed back. Then they counter-attacked and moved forward, but yet again they were repulsed.

At last, with both sides in the state of utmost fatigue, Wyndham's command made a dignified withdrawal leaving the hill in the possession of the Greys. But the rebels were unable to charge down on the Union men. They had lost too many men and were now completely worn out, too tired to make the final attack

Rutland's Blues and Greys

which the Union cavalry would have been too tired to resist.

A voice cried out, "The Colonel's wounded!"

Arthur could see a small group of horsemen, who were around Wyndham's horse, approaching from the base of the hill. As they got closer, Arthur could see that Sir Percy had been hit in the leg and was bleeding badly. They stopped his horse and lowered Wyndham to the ground. "Damned nuisance," he growled. "We had them on the run." He gesticulated to Arthur. "But didn't my boys do well? What? Damn fine show. Steady as a rock. Great fightin', what?"

"Yes, they were marvellous," smiled Arthur. "They're great fighters."

Chapter 16

Sir Percy Wyndham, who had been hit in the leg and was very weak from loss of blood, was sent back to Washington. Arthur accompanied him back to the capital and immediately on his return he headed for his rented house. Having washed, changed and had a good meal he made his way to the British Legation as he urgently wanted to know much more detail of what the military situation was.

When he saw Michael Barrington, the Ambassador's aide, he patted him on the shoulder and said, "I should have listened to you, Michael, about not joining the US Cavalry. It would have saved me a great deal of anxiety."

By mid-June General Lee had made his main move up the Shenandoah valley while being screened by the Blue Ridge Mountains. He was pushing deep into Union country, deeper than ever before, feeling the Confederates were nearer to the enemy's heart and closer to some vital part that would be a killing blow to the Union. He wanted to draw the Union Army of the Potomac out into the open for an all-out battle on ground of his choosing where he could annihilate the Northern forces.

But he was more than two hundred miles from his arsenals and supply depots, and his men were desperate for food, clothing and arms. His materiel had to be brought along unguarded roads by wagons, all of which were vulnerable to cavalry raids by the Union enemy.

By late June General Hooker was getting information from his cavalry that the Rebels were starting to move north, not towards Washington as he had feared but maybe up towards Harrisburg in Pennsylvania. To cover this he started to move the Union Army on a parallel path to where he thought the Confederates were marching, away from Washington, through Frederick and heading towards Maryland - if that was where Lee was going.

The British Legation passed on to Arthur all relevant information that they had. With the Federals moving north hoping meet Lee, Arthur decided that that was where he should be. He contacted the Union War Department and obtained permission to join up with General Hooker. Arthur eventually caught up with this enormous moving army, General Hooker's Army of the Potomac, on the outskirts of Frederick, Maryland.

It was on the road beyond Frederick, leading north-west to Hagerstown, that he found L Battery, who were in First Army Corps under Major General Reynolds, in the large Brigade gun park. As he rode into the battery position, one of the gunners recognised him and called out, "Hi, Colonel. Good to see you back."

"Glad to be back," replied Arthur as he dismounted. The gunner took his horse and he walked towards the battery command tent. Lieutenant Hasting opened the flap and stepped out. "Hallo, Colonel. I thought I heard your voice," he said as he saluted. "Good to see you, sir."

"And to see you. How are things going here?"

"Fine. Did you know we have a new BC, Captain Gilbert Reynolds?"

"Yes, we met at Fredericksburg as his brother left to go to Brigade."

"I'm afraid Captain Reynolds is not here at present. He's over with Corps HQ getting information."

Arthur looked at Charles's shoulder board with a bar on it. "I see they made you up to a full Lieutenant."

Hastings gave a wry smile. "They'd lost a number of artillery officers so they just promoted some of us."

"You're too modest, Charles. I'll bet it was on merit," smiled Arthur. "Now, what have you done with my sergeant?"

"He's over with left section. He's really fitted in with artillery life and he's learned the drill very quickly. I will be sorry to lose him. I suppose you're taking him away."

"Most certainly. I'd get in to all sorts of trouble if it wasn't for him."

Hastings pointed over towards a knot of gunners by an ammunition limber. "There he is, sir."

Arthur walked towards the group. Then Forrester saw him and quickly strode across to see him.

"Hallo, sir," he said as he saluted.

Arthur did not return the salute, holding out his hand instead. Forrester hesitated in surprise and then shook it with enthusiasm.

"It's good to have you back, sir," he said. "Where are we going to?"

Arthur laughed. "So you want to get away from the guns, do you?"

"Lord no, sir. This is the life for me. I think I might almost have earned keeping my stripes here. No, I just thought you'd be going to do something else."

"Well, Rafferty, you're right. I want to find Colonel Chamberlain and the 20th Maine. I think I'll travel with them for a time. Do you want to stay here or go with me?"

"Go with you, sir" said Forrester without any hesitation.

The Union Army was spread over many miles of road and countryside around Frederick leading north. Arthur decided that the only way to find where the 20th Maine were was to find General Hooker's HQ and ask the Staff there.

He found the HQ and was told that the 20th Maine were encamped to the north-east in the town of Westminster- but most surprisingly he found that the Senior General of the Union Army was no longer General Hooker but General Meade.

He also learned from what he picked up from the HQ staff that the Army was moving even further north and that it was shadowing, maybe even catching up with, the Confederate Army. He was also told that the

20th Maine was in the First Division of the Fifth Army Corps under Major General Sykes.

Arthur felt that he had learned a great deal about the Union gunners, and also how the Union Army was using their guns. It was obvious that the whole concept of using the artillery as a separate arm was still in turmoil and changing almost battle by battle. It appeared to be undecided who was the man in control at the time, General Hunt, a progressive thinker, or General Burnside, a bloody fool.

Arthur had tasted the Union cavalry and decided that he would not sup from that cup again. It was all too hair-raising. He therefore decided to meet up again with Lawrence Chamberlain as quickly as possible and stay with him until the coming battle was finished. If it degenerated into a long wait of army facing army, then he would reconsider whether to rejoin L Battery. He was very lucky that, whoever the General was in charge of the Union Army, he was able to get all the information required directly from that General's HQ.

It took 20 miles of riding before he and Forrester eventually found the 20th Maine camped alongside one of the roads out of Winchester leading towards Hanover.

One of the first people he saw was Colonel Chamberlain's younger brother Tom, who was now an officer.

Tom saluted Arthur. "Hallo, Colonel. Nice to see you."

"And to see you, er." He looked at the double-bar shoulder boards of a Captain. "Captain Chamberlain. Congratulations."

Rutland's Blues and Greys

Tom waved a deprecating hand. "Oh, gosh, Colonel, they promote anyone who can stand and look like an officer."

Arthur smiled in reply. "You'll do very well." He looked around at the swirling mass of infantrymen as they prepared their evening meal. "Is Colonel Chamberlain around, Captain?"

"Oh, yes, sir. I'll tell him you're here." Tom turned and ran towards an A tent set back from the Regimental office tent. Arthur smiled at the youthful enthusiasm of this young man.

The Irish corporal came up and said. "Shall I be takin' your horse then, sir."

"Thank you. It's Corporal Kilrain, isn't it?"

"Well, it was, sir, but I was in a bit of trouble, and it's Private Kilrain now."

Arthur smiled at the grizzled old soldier, who had undoubtedly had promotions and demotions all through his career in whatever army he was serving. The old Irish soldier was a gem to have around for his basic knowledge of soldiering, which would be essential for a newly made Colonel like Chamberlain.

"Colonel!" Chamberlain advanced towards Arthur with his hand outstretched.

"You are looking very fit, Lawrence. Service life obviously suits you."

Chamberlain smiled. "But not the hard ground to sleep on."

Arthur looked at Chamberlain's shoulder boards. "I see that they gave you the spread eagle of a full Colonel. Congratulations."

Lawrence smiled and said, "I assume you would like to eat with us and possibly rest with us?"

"Eat certainly. I'll bet there isn't going to be much rest, but I would like to travel with you if you would be so kind."

"It will be our pleasure. Come on and I'll find you a tent."

So Arthur joined in with the officers of the 20th Maine to eat and talk about the subjects that soldiers discuss around a campfire in the evening.

Next morning Arthur woke up to the sounds of the movement of men making ready to start on the day's march. He dressed and stepped outside his tent to see Forrester walking towards him. He also saw some commotion around a group of soldiers who were sitting under a tree looking very depressed and ragged.

Arthur noticed Kilrain walking away from the group and towards him.

Kilrain could see Arthur looking at the group of men.

"They are mutineers, sir," said Kilrain. "The Colonel is going to speak to them."

"Mutineers!"

"Yes, sir. They thought they were in for two years but they had signed on for three years - when the others were allowed to go home, the three-year men mutinied. They have been brought up here to the 20th and the Colonel has been told to take them over or shoot them."

"Shoot them!" exclaimed Arthur. "Surely he wouldn't do that."

Rutland's Blues and Greys

"Lord no, your Honour. The Colonel won't be doing that. He's given them some food and he is going to talk to them, but the regiment is going to lead off shortly. They'd told him that they hadn't eaten for some time so he said that he'd get them some meat. One man came out from the group and spoke to the Colonel, who has taken him to his tent. Presumably he's tellin' the Colonel of the men's grievances now."

Arthur turned to Forrester. "Get our horses, Sergeant, and I'll try and get us some food."

A number of bugles were calling around the area as the neighbouring regiments prepared for the day's march.

Arthur managed to get two mugs of coffee plus some hard tack and cheese. By the time he got back to his tent Forrester was there with the horses, which he hitched to a nearby line. The two men ate their food and drank their coffee while waiting for the 20th Maine to break camp.

Arthur noticed a ragged soldier come out of the Colonel's tent and walk towards the main group of men. Shortly afterwards he was followed by Chamberlain.

"Stay here with the horses, Sergeant," Arthur said to Forrester, and he walked towards the gathering of men, who were still sitting or lying down. He kept well back against a tree and watched Lawrence approach the group of mutineers. His head was low, his chin down on his chest; he was obviously deep in thought.

'How is he going to be able to do anything in just a few minutes?' thought Arthur. 'Surely it's impossible'.

The men were sitting looking sullenly at Chamberlain. None of them got up as he approached - then quietly he started to talk.

Arthur slowly moved closer until he could hear properly what Lawrence was saying. Here was a Professor of Debate and Rhetoric trying to influence honest and true men, who were certain that they had a valid complaint, but who the Army considered to be mutineers.

Chamberlain did not use big words or stirring phrases. He did not give wild impossible promises, he just spoke as one man from Maine to these other men from Maine.

Arthur watched the men carefully, and listened to the words. Then he could gradually see the overt hatred and sullenness start to lessen. Chamberlain told them he could promise nothing except that he was never going to shoot them, and that he would put their case to the senior General. But first the 20th Maine were going to fight a battle and extra men to replace his casualties were badly wanted.

He told them that the regiment had formed last year, and that only half of the original men were left but these veterans were quality men. He said he couldn't give them good reasons to fight, but when last year "we all started up we thought it was the right thing to do."

"This is a country of free choice, free to live where you want and do what you want - but we are all fighting for each other's right to do just that". They could come and fight if they wanted to or they would come and stay under an armed guard. There was no threat in this, just a statement of the facts.

"We are all in this army, and you can choose. You can have your rifles back and fight with us or come along under guard. You've only got a few minutes to decide as we must be heading the column. You'll have my sincere personal thanks if you do choose to fight with us." There was complete silence as he finished. Then he turned away and walked slowly back to his Regimental staff.

It was masterly! At the end Arthur felt an incredible admiration for this amateur soldier who, through his professionalism, knew exactly how to use a common language to communicate to these honest men, and he showed them that he understood their needs and their feelings.

Arthur walked back to where Sergeant Forrester was holding the horses. Both men mounted and rode in silence as they slowly caught up and joined some officers in the centre of the 20th Maine, who were already marching up the road to Hanover. A short time later Lawrence Chamberlain trotted his horse up to the head of the column and led the Regiment as it marched along to its new position.

Arthur decided to stay back from the lead while Chamberlain sorted out his immediate instructions and the problem of the mutineers.

After a while, Chamberlain's brother Tom trotted his horse up to the Colonel and spoke animatedly to him. Lawrence made some comment and then Tom trotted back down the column. He saw Arthur and pulled his horse over to ride alongside. "Wow, Colonel, did you ever see anything like that?"

"How many have chosen to join you?" asked Arthur.

"The whole dang lot 'cept two or three. The whole dang lot! So many that we haven't got enough rifles for them all." Tom slapped his thigh and said to Arthur, "Wasn't he good?"

"He was incredible." Arthur shook his head in disbelief. "He was - incredible."

Arthur eventually moved up to the front of the column, and manoeuvred himself to ride beside Chamberlain. Sergeant Forrester followed a few yards behind.

Lawrence turned his head as though coming out of deep thought.

"Hello, Arthur."

"Hello, Lawrence."

For a while the two men rode in silence, then Arthur said, "Theoretically, Lawrence, I, as the professional soldier, should be able to teach you a great deal in the ways of the military, but…" He paused. "An hour ago you showed me that I have a great deal to learn about how to handle men." Again he paused. "Those men, who are not strictly trained soldiers but who are thinking men, had an understandable and serious grievance - yet you won their hearts."

Lawrence turned his head and smiled. "Thank you, Arthur. From you that is a compliment indeed."

Again the two men rode in silence, but gradually they started to talk about many subjects. The professional officer and the amateur volunteer, the Professor of Rhetoric and an attentive student. They talked easily, these two men who were so similar yet so different, both professionals of high quality, who had become sound friends.

The march was through northern Maryland and across the state line into the rolling countryside of Pennsylvania. The column marched along the dusty road under the hot sun until they reached the town of Hanover. There were virtually no stragglers as this regiment was now made up of veteran and hardened infantry. They marched through Hanover and onto the Baltimore Pike, which was leading towards a small town called Gettysburg.

Through the villages along the road crowds of people came to their front gates to welcome this northern army. They had not had the Rebels pass through and so did not know the fear of requisitioning.

Fruit, bread and milk were all offered to the men as they marched along the road.

One buxom woman standing outside her garden called to Arthur. "Would you like some hot rolls, General?"

Forrester quickly said, "I'll get them, sir."

"No," teased Arthur. "The lady offered them to me." He rode over and leaned down to take two large crispy bread rolls filled with butter and cheese. "That's excellent, madam. Thank you very much." The woman was obviously nonplussed by Arthur's accent and just said. "Not at all, sir."

Then from the north came the sound of a deep rumbling. It wavered up and down in the hot air.

"That's strange," said the woman. "It doesn't look like rain, sir, but that thunder sounds very heavy. Never heard it like that afore."

Arthur had lifted his head to ensure he was correct before he said to her, "That's gunfire, madam."

The woman looked up at him in amazement and said, "Oh, my Lord, what cannons and things?"

Arthur nodded.

"Oh, my Lord!" she cried. Then she turned and scurried back indoors, slamming her front door loudly and very firmly.

Arthur listened again, the guns were not that far away and there seemed to be a large number of them. He rode back to the column and gave one of the rolls to Forrester.

Chapter 17

Arthur walked beside his horse and continued to listen to the gunfire as the regiment marched along. Eventually, when he thought the action was only a mile or so ahead, he saw a senior officer come cantering down the road towards the head of the column. It was Colonel Vincent, the Brigade commander. He reined his horse in and spoke urgently to Chamberlain, who called his officers to him.

Colonel Vincent rode out to the left and shouted out "Column of fours. Follow me!" The regiment swung left and then trotted across fields until they reached a road which Arthur was told was the Taneytown Road leading to Gettysburg, where they were heading. On the left of the road a steep slope rose to the top of a small hill, which appeared to be on the end of the main ridge.

Colonel Vincent stood up in his stirrups and yelled again. He swung his arm to show that the regiment was wanted up the slope - and they were wanted urgently. The infantrymen, scrambling and running, quickly found tracks that led up to the top.

Arthur wondered what was happening up there, and what could be seen from the top of the small hill.

"Sergeant, I'm just going up that slope," he said." I'll be back in a few minutes."

"But, sir..."

"Sergeant, just hold my horse down here for a few minutes."

Arthur dismounted and scrambled with the infantry up the rocky slope of Little Round Top from the Taneytown Road. As he reached the crest, he could see men running forward through the thin cover of trees to form a defensive line in the woods behind stone walls and some large logs that were scattered about. Instantly, they started to fire at targets that were well beyond Arthur's view.

He turned to walk back down the slope when he heard a shout "Colonel!" He turned to see Colonel Vincent, the senior Union officer, gesturing, not to him, but to Lawrence.

The officer called to Chamberlain, "You must hold this line including the far left. You are the end of the Army line. You must not be pushed off this hill - it'll turn the whole of the Army!" Chamberlain saluted in response and ran back to his lines of men and their officers.

Arthur looked up as the trees seemed to be full of bees whipping by. The Rebels' bullets were cutting the foliage and branches out of the trees, which fell on the 20th Maine, as well as cutting down its men.

Arthur walked in a crouch back to the top of the Little Round Top, and looking down he could see the lines of grey and butternut uniformed men pushing up

Rutland's Blues and Greys

the slope towards him. There were masses of them, far too many for the remaining men of the 20th to repulse. The Federal soldiers would now certainly be swamped unless there could be some support but there was none coming from off the Taneytown Road. He turned again to walk back down to the road, but he knew he could not go - he had to help in the smallest way. He had to help these men who he had come to know and respect. He looked at the low wall just in front of him and saw the body of a dead Federal soldier slumped with his rifle beside him. Arthur ran over in a crouch until he reached the wall. He pulled the dead body away and took up the man's rifle and opened his cartridge pouch. There were about 15 rounds in it. Then he checked that the rifle had been fired and took one of the paper cartridges from the pouch. He tore off the end with his teeth, poured the powder down the barrel, turned the cartridge over to put the Minie in and rammed it down. He reached across to the man's cap pouch, pulled back the flap and took out a number of percussion caps. He put them into his jacket pocket but fitted one on the rifle's nipple. Pulling back the hammer fully, he aimed the rifle over the wall at the first grey uniform he could see – and fired. The grey uniform, fifty yards away, slammed back with a large red hole torn in the chest.

Lying behind the wall, Arthur took another round from the pouch, loaded and rammed it, fumbled in his pocket for a cap, then aimed at another Grey and fired. Again the man fell back – dead. He loaded, rammed, capped and fired again and again until there were only a couple of rounds left in the dead man's pouch. It was then that Arthur realised he must have fired about a dozen rounds - and possibly twelve men had died.

The strong Rebel charge had been repulsed, but from the movement of figures back in the scrub it looked as though they were gathering together for yet another attack. He started to load again when he heard a call from Lawrence Chamberlain for his officers.

Chamberlain, realising that the regiment could not stand even one more attack from the Rebels because they were almost out of ammunition, had decided to take the attack to them. He called out to his officers that he would order the men to give a bayonet charge down the slope with his left wing swinging to the right like a door shutting. This would mean the Rebels would be held in the front and then hit from the side. It was a reckless idea but almost the only way out of a disastrous situation.

The officers having received their orders dispersed back to their posts. Arthur raised his head from the rifle and looked up at Lawrence, who was standing on the wall a few yards away, his sword held in his hand. Then, at the top of his voice, Chamberlain shouted just one word. "BAY-ON-ETS!"

The Colonel paused while his men drew their bayonets from their scabbards and fixed them on to the end of their rifles. In those few seconds, as the regiment prepared for the charge, he glanced down at Arthur, who was still in the firing position behind the wall. But Arthur knew he could not take part in a bayonet charge. To defend one's friends against an overwhelming attack was one thing, but to fight with them in a bayonet charge and the hand-to-hand fighting was just not possible.

Chamberlain looked to left and right; he saw his men were as ready as they were ever going to be. Then raising his sword above his head, he shouted at the top of his voice "CHARGE!" His officers took up the cry, which was immediately followed by the shouts and roars of all of those men from Maine.

Arthur watched as the men in blue rose up, almost without any ammunition, and threw themselves in an unstoppable mass down the slope at the men in grey.

He rested his head on his arms that were still holding the rifle. He heard the cries of the charge and then the screams of the wounded and dying. It tore at his mind – his conscience - his very soul, and it hurt him badly.

Arthur raised his head, peered over the low wall and saw that the fierce fighting had swept down to the bottom of the hill. He suddenly realised that he had a terrible thirst, caused from biting off the cartridges, which made him reach for his canteen of water. He pulled out the cork and put the container to his lips. He felt the warm water cascade over his tongue and wash the sulphurous taste of the black powder from his mouth. He swallowed and swallowed – and stopped. There must be many wounded out there who wanted water much more than he did.

Wearily he stood up and slowly walked down the hill; halfway down he came across the first of the wounded. Some wore blue and some wore grey. He straightened out a number who were incapable of moving their broken and torn limbs and gave them just a mouthful of water if their own canteen was empty.

One of the grey uniformed men was quietly trying to raise himself up. Arthur went over and saw a terrible wound in the left side of the man's chest.

"Lie still," he said. "The medical men will come shortly. Would you like a little water?" The man nodded and Arthur raised the canteen so that some water could pour into the man's mouth.

"Are you from England ?" the Grey asked.

"Yes."

"You must be the Colonel that Dan'l spoke about. We sure liked your fancy ceegars."

Arthur smiled. "I'm glad about that. How is Daniel?"

The man coughed, and blood poured from his mouth. He wiped his sleeve across his lips as though nothing was amiss. "I ain't for certain sure but I know he's with Pickett's Brigade so he's prob'ly alright." More blood flowed from his mouth and dribbled down his chin. He coughed again and then with his eyes still focused on Arthur's, the soldier's whole face and body gradually relaxed; slowly it slumped closer to the earth as his life gently and irrevocably drained away. As the Grey's body slumped to the ground, Arthur closed the man's eyes - then he bowed his head while a terrible anguish tore at him. Kneeling beside the still warm body he tried to say a prayer for this unknown man, something to mark his death, anything – but nothing came.

"Help me. Oh please, will someone help me!"

Arthur heard the innocent, plaintive cry and looked up to see a Confederate soldier, a young man, almost a boy, lying on his side twenty yards away - but heavy

Rutland's Blues and Greys

bleeding was showing from the right chest and the lad's arm was badly mangled. Terrible anguish was on the young soldier's muddy face. "Please help me."

Arthur scrambled over and knelt down by the lad's side. "Relax, the surgeons will come soon." As he poured water onto the muddy lips, Arthur could see a large pool of blood beside the Grey's hip. He had also been hit in an artery there.

The lad blinked at Arthur and lay back on the ground. "Will you write to my ma? I know I'm agonna die but I want her to know that I was thinkin' 'bout her an' that I warn't sceered."

"Yes, son," said Arthur. "I'll write to her. Now lie still." He stood up, pulled out his gunner's pad and a pencil, then he knelt again beside the boy.

"What's your name, soldier?"

"I'm Private Nathaniel Matherson, sir."

Arthur wrote the name down in the pad and said, "Where are you from?" But in the time it had taken to have his name written down, Private Nathaniel Matherson had quietly and gently died. Arthur looked at the ashen skin of the boy's face that told of the massive loss of blood that had poured from his wounds, taking his life, and all of his future, to seep into the blood-sodden ground of that little hill at Gettysburg. Arthur closed the lad's eyes and suddenly remembered the Irish lad at Fredericksburg repeating "Hail Mary, full of Grace." Had the prayer worked for him? If so, why had God decided that he should live and Nathaniel should die - or was the son of Erin now also just clay like this young rebel?

Kneeling beside the body, Arthur felt an awful depression gradually flow over him.

'I've become too involved,' he thought. 'I'm treating all of them like my family - my gunners.' Slowly he got to his feet and shook the water bottle. It was almost empty. With his head bowed, he turned and started to walk back up the Little Round Top. Behind him he could hear the cries of the wounded, both Blues and Greys, but he did not stop. He was walking away from them all. He left behind there part of his soul; it was back there in torment, crying with them and for them.

As he slowly stumbled up the slope of the small hill, a Union Infantry Sergeant strode past him. "We sure gave 'em a licking, Colonel."

Arthur nodded.

"Hell," continued the Sergeant, "I'd be willin' to do that agin every day of the week."

Arthur could understand the man's exhilaration; an hour ago he did not know if he was going to survive the fight or killed by the Rebels. 'Yes, I understand,' he thought. 'half an hour ago you didn't know if you would be alive - and now you are triumphant because you are alive.'

He reached the stone wall that he had been kneeling behind when the attacks came, and saw the dead private whose rifle he had used, but Arthur did not stop. He walked on towards the crest.

"Colonel!"

Arthur looked up to see a corporal from the 20th Maine calling to him. "Here's your sergeant."

"My sergeant?" asked Arthur.

"Yes, sir, your shadow, the one who's always with you."

"Forrester! Where?"

"Here, sir, by this rock." The Corporal pointed to the ground. "I'm afraid he's dead, sir."

Arthur could see, ahead of him, the dark-blue clad body of a Federal soldier slumped against a log. Stumbling up the slope towards it, he felt his stomach tearing in anguish. 'He mustn't be dead.' But as he got closer he could see that indeed it was Forrester, his body slumped alongside a large log, with blood from the terrible lethal head wound spread across his face.

'Oh God,' Arthur prayed fervently. A horrendous terror swamped him. 'Not him, not Rafferty.'

Arthur knelt down beside the sergeant's body and gently turned him onto his back.

"Oh Rafferty, why…. Why did you follow me?" Arthur spoke softly to himself but also to this loyal friend who had been beside him for so many months.

The large fatal wound in the head above the ear had spread blood across Rafferty's ashen face. More blood dribbled from the wound and Arthur felt for his handkerchief to staunch it.

Blood flowing! If his blood is flowing, maybe he is alive! Arthur held Rafferty's wrist and felt for a pulse. Yes! It was very faint but there was one. He pulled at the Sergeant's jacket and lifted him up slightly to prop him up against the tree log. He slowly trickled the last of the water over Rafferty's lips and then gradually into his mouth. There was no response - and then he swallowed!

Arthur stood up and looked around. A dead Union soldier lay a few feet away with his water canteen still across his shoulder. Arthur lifted it up and felt that it was half full. He pulled the strap over the dead man's shoulder and scrambled back to the sergeant.

He poured water from the canteen over Forrester's wound and saw under the congealed blood that it was a ragged tear along the side of his head. He had also lost the top half of his ear, and it was that which appeared to be producing most of the blood. Arthur stood up and felt inside his jacket to the two special pockets. Then he pulled out his Millie pack of pads and bandages and opened it up. He took one pad, pressed it against the sergeant's wound and bound it on with a bandage around his head.

Again he gently raised Rafferty's head and poured water across his lips allowing some to trickle into his mouth. With his wet handkerchief he washed more of the blood off Rafferty's face – then he saw an eyelid move and at last Rafferty opened his eyes.

"Damn you, Sergeant," choked Arthur. "You had me scared stiff then."

Forrester looked up at Arthur dazedly. "Colonel?"

"Yes, Sergeant. You're meant to be looking after me, not the other way round."

"I'm... I'm sorry, sir."

"So am I, Rafferty," said Arthur gently. "I'm so very sorry." He stood up. "I'll find some help to get you down to the hospital."

"No, I'll be alright if you could just bind up my leg."

"Your leg!" Arthur looked at the sergeant's right leg and saw a bloody tear in the material. Arthur got out his pocket knife and started to cut away the trousers. "What the hell were you doing up here? I left you down on the road with the horses."

"I came up to get you away from the dangerous part, sir. Then I saw you take up the rifle and I thought, that's what I should be doing." He winced as Arthur pulled the cloth open to look at the wound in his thigh. Though a large wound, it was on the outside and had torn a slash through the flesh and muscle. It looked as though the bleeding had mainly stopped. Arthur pulled out the other pad from his Millie pack.

"I was doing alright until Colonel Chamberlain called for the bayonet charge. I started off with them but got hit in the leg. And then I must have been hit in the head, but I don't remember that."

As Arthur bound the pad against the leg wound, he said with a trembling voice, "Sergeant, you're a bloody fool, a marvellous, courageous, loyal, bloody fool."

Rafferty smiled. "I must've learnt that from you, sir."

Arthur looked up and into the Sergeant's eyes, then with a paternal gesture, gently put his hand against the side of Rafferty's face. "I think we're good for each other," he said. "Come on, put your arm around my shoulder and let's get you standing up."

The two soldiers, one sergeant and one colonel, slowly made their way down towards the track leading to the Taneytown Road, which ran behind the defensive ridge and towards the centre of the Federal position. There, they found both of their horses still there, tethered to some scrub. Arthur got Forrester's sound leg into a stirrup and lifted him up into the saddle. Then he mounted his own horse and they both slowly rode towards the hospital area in the Headquarters of the Army of the Potomac.

By the time they reached the emergency aid area, Arthur had made up his mind. From now on he would stay well to the rear and he would not become involved, especially as his actions had endangered Forrester's life. Come what may, he would definitely not become involved anymore.

Chapter 18

Next morning as soon as Arthur woke, he got out of his blankets and then splashed water in his face to wake himself fully. He opened his saddle pack, pulled out his binoculars and swung the case strap over his shoulder. He was only going to study any of the fighting that day from a distance where he could use them. Then he noticed his Field Staff cap with its red band. He pulled it out, pushed it into a reasonable shape and decided to wear it. 'I'm staying away from the fighting so I'll wear my proper uniform.'

He lifted up his worn and faded Union Artillery cap and carefully removed the Royal Artillery Grenade badge. He put the badge into his jacket pocket and pushed the Union cap back into his saddle pack

Lifting the flap of his tent, he strode quickly towards the hospital area, which was a few hundred yards away. He found Rafferty, who was lying on the ground with dozens of the other wounded. He was asleep and covered by a blanket. Arthur looked around and saw, close by, the same Lieutenant Medical Officer who had treated Rafferty the day before. Arthur gestured him over.

"Can I help, Colonel?"

"How is he?" Arthur pointed towards Forrester.

The surgeon knelt down, pulled back the blanket and looked at the bandage on Rafferty's leg.

"As long as he doesn't get an infection in the wound, he'll be fine in a few weeks' time. It was a bad tear, but we cleaned it up very well, so there is every chance he'll recover fully. The head wound was bloody but not serious."

"Thank you."

"There are Letterman's ambulances going back to Westminster, where trains are taking wounded back to Baltimore and Washington all the time. He'll be on one in the next hour or so."

"I would be very grateful if you'd ensure that he did leave for a hospital as quickly as possible."

"I'll see that he does, sir."

Forrester had woken when his blanket was pulled off him. He looked up at Arthur. "Good morning, Colonel."

Arthur smiled "Good morning, Sergeant." He knelt down on one knee and adjusted the blanket back to cover Forrester's legs. "The surgeon says you'll be fine. Just make sure that the wound is kept clean. Don't let anyone wash it with dirty or bloody water."

"Right, sir."

"They'll get you away in an ambulance and then back by train to a hospital nearer to Washington very soon, so you'll be in safe hands shortly."

"And you, sir?"

"Me?"

"Yes, sir. Will you be in safe hands when I've gone back?"

Arthur smiled at the sergeant. "Yes," he said. "Look, I've got my binoculars with me. I'll only be watching from a distance."

"Please make sure you do, Colonel."

Arthur gripped Forrester's shoulder. "Don't you worry about me, Rafferty. You made me see some good sense yesterday. I'll keep safe."

"Colonel, could I ask a favour of you?"

"Certainly, what is it?"

"Could you let me have something, just something small, that will remind me of us meeting. Something that one day I can show my son and say this belonged to an English officer I served with."

"A memento. Most certainly. I have the perfect thing." He stood up and took out the Royal Artillery Flaming Grenade cap badge from his pocket. "Here, this is for you. You have surely earned it."

Forrester took the badge, and looked up at him. "Goodbye, sir. I've enjoyed being your shadow, 'n I've learnt a lot. I hope we meet again."

"So do I, Rafferty," said Arthur looking down at the man for whom he had developed a very deep affection. He drew himself to attention and gave a sharp formal salute. "Goodbye, First Sergeant," he said.

Rafferty smiled, showing a mutual feeling. "Goodbye, sir"

Arthur turned to walk back towards the General's Headquarters. As he did so, he heard Rafferty call softly after him. "Take care, Colonel. Take care."

Arthur slightly turned his head and gently raised his hand in a small acknowledgement of having heard. The emotion of the parting was too great. He couldn't turn round and look back at the man he considered as a younger brother - or even a son.

"You take care too, Rafferty," he whispered. "Take great care."

General Lee was certain he knew where the Union line was now at its weakest. He had hit them hard on their right flank above Gettysburg town on the first day. This he followed the next day with a strong attack on the Union left wing at the Little Round Top. He would keep up pressure on these two points, but he would send in his main attack against the Union centre which was running along Cemetery Ridge.

The ridge had a clear approach across a wide open field with just a few wooden fences crossing it. The Emmitsburg Road bisected the approach, but this would not affect the advancing regiments. The ridge was also clear of scrub and trees except for a small cluster of trees right on the crest, exactly in the middle. It was a perfect mark or aiming point for his army to head for and converge on.

Lee's instructions to Longstreet, the General in charge of the right wing, were that he was to attack towards the clump of trees on the top of Cemetery Ridge. He told Longstreet to precede the advance with the army's massed guns and to make sure they gave cover during the advance.

Rutland's Blues and Greys

Arthur walked behind the Union defences and up to the top of the ridge. A small cluster of trees formed a mark for him to stop at. He scanned the field from left to right, and saw that the Union lines were very strong with many infantrymen crouching behind stonewalls or improvised lines of logs and boulders. The Union guns were spread all along the front face of the ridge, which he had found out was called Cemetery Ridge.

He scanned the Union lines from well over to the left in front of the battleground of the day before, Little Round Top, to the far right wing which appeared to be on a bend of the hills above Gettysburg, the little town below him and to his right. The town was obviously in Confederate hands and was the shelter for any Rebel attack.

He swung his glasses across the field in front of him to the woods opposite where the Confederate army was situated. Then he started to see the amazing sight of masses of Confederate artillery pouring out of the woods and being arranged at the foot of the ridge opposite, in front of the woods some 1500 odd yards away. They were lining themselves up obviously preparatory to an enormous barrage. The rebel attack was going to come straight at the centre of the Federal line across open fields and across the Emmitsburg Road which ran between both armies' positions. The Confederate artillery would have a very tricky job to maintain heavy fire on the Union positions while the infantry advanced right up to the moment they charged some 200 yards from the Union lines. It was going to be essential as without it the infantry would be at the mercy of the

Federal artillery and infantry's rifles for a long time over completely open ground.

'No,' thought Arthur. 'That is impossible. It is going to be very interesting to see how good the Confederate Artillery Commander is in controlling the gun support for the last few yards.'

Arthur watched in growing amazement at the arranging of the Confederate forces. There was no attempt to hide the fact that there was going to be a frontal attack straight up the slope towards the Cemetery Ridge. This left time for the Federal forces to arrange themselves to defend this position at their leisure – but why was there no counter battery fire from the Federal artillery? The target was there, plain to see. It was within range, so why were the guns not firing?

Arthur lowered his glasses and looked around at the batteries close to him. None were taking any action; they were all just watching – and presumably waiting for the attack.

A group of half a dozen high ranking officers cantered up in front of Arthur. He could see that one was General Hunt, and he was looking through his binoculars at the rebel guns, moving his view from left to right. He lowered his glasses picked up his reins and turned his horse up the hill to pass close to Arthur.

As the General trotted by, he looked at Arthur, who saluted him.

"So, Colonel," called Hunt. "At last someone has decided to mass his guns." He turned his horse's head towards Arthur. "I expect you're not over surprised that it's happened."

"No, General."

Hunt, who was now quite close to Arthur, looked down at him and quietly said, "I expect also that you're wondering why we are not firing at such a grand target."

"Well, actually, General, I am rather surprised."

Hunt gently beckoned Arthur to come closer, then bent down and said, "I believe in saving ammunition for the advancing infantry and not waste it on their guns. But watch our guns on the flanks. They will be having good target practice shortly." He paused and looked again at the rebel guns. Then he turned to Arthur and said quietly, "Also I'm not certain I've got enough ammunition."

Arthur felt a look of shock fly across his face.

Hunt looked down and nodded. "Between you and me, Colonel, between you and me." He turned his horse up towards the top of the slope.

Arthur pulled out his gunner's pad and started to sketch the scene before him. Having got the basic background in the correct proportion, he started to count the number of cannon being placed there. He could see round to his left front, guns placed in the valley pointed to cover the attack from the Rebel left flank. But to his front and, as far as he could see, to his right there were an incredible long line of massed guns. Arthur realised that this was the largest mass of guns preparing to fire in anger that he had ever seen – and they were pointed at him!

He started to count. From the rising ground to the left, across the open valley and then along the ridge opposite, stretching parallel to the ridge on which he was standing, then over to the right in front of Gettysburg itself there must have been around one hundred and sixty guns!

He looked around at the Federal gun positions around him; they were all near the top of the ridge. Why isn't General Hunt or Meade pulling back half of his artillery to a safe position behind and just below the ridge top? The old Duke of Wellington would have done that to save his artillery and his infantry - but then of course he was dealing with highly trained soldiery. Here, if you pulled back alternate regiments until the bombardment was over, the rest of the Union soldiers might well wonder why they were left out there in danger, and decide to retire also, which would result in great confusion. These men were tough and very brave, but it needed strict discipline to stand fast when those around you had gone to safety.

It was about midday and lunchtime that Arthur was sitting at the table eating with General Meade's staff when he saw Lawrence Chamberlain, with his wounded leg, hobbling past the tented area. He looked incredibly tired and gaunt. Arthur got up, went through to the cooks' section, where he picked up a whole cooked chicken and walked out through the flap of the kitchen tent. He could see Lawrence still limping below the top of the ridge. Arthur trotted over to him.

" Lawrence, how are you?"

"Oh, tired."

"And hungry?"

"Yes, hungry."

Arthur handed him the chicken. "I'm sorry I didn't stay with you after the battle."

Chamberlain shook his head. "Arthur, you shouldn't have been there in the first place but thank you for your help – for your support. The men saw it and they were grateful – as I am." He looked so tired that he might have fallen down any minute.

Arthur put his hand on Lawrence's arm "For goodness sake, go and have a rest. Your men are in reserve, resting, and so should you be. If you're exhausted, you won't be of much use when the attack comes. Your men might be needed."

"You're certain they'll attack?"

Arthur nodded. "I've watched the build-up of their artillery and I'm certain they will come straight at this position."

"Here?" queried Chamberlain.

"Yes, here. There are some one hundred and fifty guns lined up to start at any moment. Now go and rest. When the bombardment starts, ignore it for an hour or so. Your regiment won't be called before then."

"How do you know?" asked Chamberlain.

Arthur smiled. "Because I'm a professional soldier – I just know." He put his hand on Lawrence 's shoulder and gave a little push. "Now go and rest."

Chamberlain turned and, as though in a trance, walked slowly down the hill towards the remains of his regiment.

Arthur took out his handkerchief, wiped the chicken grease off his hands and turned to walk up the hill. At the crest he walked over to the small clump of trees. He took out his notebook and looked at his sketch of the battlefield. It was generally correct so he snapped it shut and through his glasses looked closely at the array of guns again.

Then it started! Two separate bangs. Obviously the signal for the barrage to commence. A rippling burst of smoke flowed along the line of guns, which instantly turned in to a blast of sound. This was inevitably changed into flying metal slamming into the Federal lines. The air was a hell, full of screaming metal as Lee's artillery started its bombardment of the Union lines and artillery.

Arthur moved back into the clump of trees, stood behind the largest one and looked down at the line of Southern guns and the enveloping clouds of smoke. They were using artillery as it was meant to be used, but they had not done any ranging to start with. How did they know all their guns had the correct elevation?

Arthur watched the incoming shells and shot – some hit the defended area but some were well short and others flew over the crest. It all spoke of keen amateur enthusiasm but an incredible lack of technical expertise.

Arthur looked behind him and down into the valley - the Union men and guns could still be moved on the Taneytown Road down there without being hurt.

Some of the Federal guns were now replying but they could easily waste ammunition now when their target area was covered in gun smoke. There was no way to check if they were hitting what they were aiming at.

As the hail of metal screamed around him, Arthur decided to run back and lie down just below the edge of the slope out of the fall of shot. He had lain there for about thirty minutes when he realised that even more shells were flying over him and falling into the valley behind. He got up and again ran forward to the clump of trees to stand behind the largest one. There was still the same amount of smoke coming from the same line of guns but – then it dawned on him what was happening.

He heard a voice say, "So, Colonel, General Lee has taken your advice and massed his artillery against us." Arthur looked round to see General Hancock seated on a horse.

Arthur saluted and said, "But his top gunner is making a very basic mistake, sir."

"What's that?" asked Hancock.

"Not checking the fall of shot. The barrels are getting hotter. It all means the shot is gradually flying higher and over the crest."

"You mean I'm safe up here?" asked Hancock looking down from his saddle with a smile.

"If you got off your horse, you'd be even safer, sir."

"There are times, Colonel, when a General must be seen riding along the lines."

Hancock looked through his field glasses at the Rebel lines.

"Is your friend down there, sir?" asked Arthur.

Hancock nodded. "I fear so. That's Pickett's Brigade. Yes, I fear he's down there."

He looked down at Arthur, who nodded in understanding. Then the General turned his horse to ride down towards the rows of infantry up against the defensive stone walls and fences.

Arthur watched the General as he rode down to his men, and then he realised that because the infantry were well below the top of the ridge they were not being hit as much as the guns who were behind them nearer the top.

Over to his right he could see some batteries of 3-inch ordnance rifle guns firing at the Confederate guns. They seemed to be firing with great care, ensuring that their target was being hit.

He lifted his glasses and spied some more 3-inch guns on Little Round Top also using converging shooting to hit the Southern guns. As he watched them, he gradually realised that all of the Union guns near to him were no longer firing. Were they out of ammunition or waiting for the attack? Eventually, after over an hour and a half the Southern guns also fell silent, and gradually the gun smoke drifted away to reveal the whole valley in front of him.

Arthur used his glasses to inspect the damage done to the Union defences. As he scanned the lines, he saw to his amazement that, though the Union artillery had taken a lot of damage, the main lines of infantry defences slightly further forward down the slope did not seem to have been hurt much. It all proved that it was wrong to assume that heavy gunfire would destroy the enemy - it had to fall in the correct place to do that.

Chapter 19

Arthur raised the view of his field glasses and scrutinised the opposite ridge. Where were the Confederate infantry? He swept the line of trees and, looking carefully, he noticed a movement behind the guns. There they were, back there in the woods, and now they were coming out! The Southern masses started to pour out in groups and lines, regiments and battalions. They kept on streaming out of the shadow of the trees, regiment by regiment, and eventually lined up into an incredibly large attacking force.

Gradually, they formed themselves up and Arthur could see the different attack forces. He took out his notebook and again sketched the divisions lined up. By doing that he could assess the number of men in each group and so multiply them up until he came to the whole total. It was an astounding 14,000 men or possibly even more!

The Confederate infantrymen all stood for some time patiently waiting for their final orders. Arthur raised his field glasses again to see the regimental officers issuing last instructions and then lining the men so that they attacked as a consolidated offensive group. The Southern Army seemed to be an enormous grey line with the spotted contrast of butternut spread amongst them. Hats of all shades and shapes sat on the heads of the soldiery. Rifles rested on their shoulders, with their bayonets already fixed.

This was an enormous swamping mass of infantry that could well sweep the Union army off the ridge. With simple artillery support the Confederates should win the day.

The whole Confederate front had to be at least one mile wide. Were they really hoping to swamp a whole mile of Union defences – or... Arthur lowered his glasses to think - to think the almost impossible. Had General Lee told his commanders to start with a one mile front - but then for the wings to merge in echelon towards the centre so that a completely unstoppable mass of infantry with incredible depth would annihilate the Union defences? With his glasses he scanned the scene and started to count the actual regimental flags. There were some fifty different regiments, all lined up to hit the spot in front of him!

Arthur quickly considered what he should do when the Greys swamped the Union lines. He decided that he would have time to run down the slope behind him and reach his horse, which was already saddled at General Meade's HQ, and then he should be able to get clear of the rear lines of Cemetery Ridge using the Taneytown Road towards Frederick. All that would work as long as there was not a mass of fleeing Union soldiers. He decided that he would move very promptly when he saw that the Confederates were about to break the Union lines.

The panorama that was now formed across the valley was utterly breathtaking. It was as though these men were on the parade ground as they stepped forward on their journey to destiny. Within a few minutes Arthur's surmise was confirmed. He watched as the brigades gradually started to manoeuvre from the wings into a tighter force in the centre.

It was now that the Union artillery started to cough out their packets of death. Shot and shell tore terrible strips into the advancing horde, and scarlet lanes were blown into the slowly advancing rebels.

Arthur looked beyond the advancing infantry towards the Confederate guns; they would be firing any moment now in support. Maybe if they were very accurate, they could wait a few moments longer so that their infantry would be that amount closer.

Then the Rebels came to the fences in the fields that edged the Emmitsburg road. While tearing them down, the Greys stopped and the Union guns slammed more and more shot into the ever-thickening mass.

Having crossed the road, the Confederates started up the steeper part of the hillside and the Union guns changed to shrapnel and canister to smash more men into eternity as bloody heaps.

Still there was no fire from the Rebel guns! Why? They couldn't be out of ammunition, could they? They could not leave it much longer otherwise they would be endangering their own men.

Obviously the centre of the Confederate attack was the Union line exactly where Arthur stood. In fact as he looked around there was only one marking point on the hill, and that was the very group of trees he was standing in.

As they gradually and painfully closed, one senior Rebel officer, leading a large attack group, took off his large black hat and, putting it on the tip of his sword, held it above his head. It was his own rallying sign. He was showing his men that he was there in the lead and he expected them to follow.

Arthur wondered if General Hancock's close friend Lewis Armistead was down there. Was he leading a brigade? Would he be alive at the end?

But why hadn't the Southern gunners fired over their heads? They had to be out of ammunition?

It had been perfect for the Rebel guns. They had ranged reasonably well with their barrage to start with. The time to fire over their infantry's heads was when they were about half of the way.

Where were the guns?

This was like Fredericksburg except there was one large wave of men advancing over open ground without any artillery support, yet all the time they were being slaughtered by shot, shell and rifle fire

In horror Arthur remembered Charles Hastings' cry at Fredericksburg. "Where were the bloody guns?"

Just below him the treble lines of dark blue uniformed Union soldiers crouched behind their flimsy defence line of stone walls or fencing posts and rails. They must have wondered, just as Arthur did, if they could hold back this enormous Confederate tidal wave which was now just a few hundred yards away.

Rutland's Blues and Greys

Then the massed Union infantry fired! A thick line of powder smoke masked the front, but Arthur being higher than the soldiers saw the effect of the lead bullets as they tore into the massed rebels.

But still the Rebels came on! Another hundred yards and they would be in with the bayonet and overrun the trenches. So the Rebels started their blood-chilling Yell. It tore across the field and lifted the spirits of the Greys - they knew they could do it! But Union rifle fire and the canister of the guns were spreading blood and flesh all over the slope of the aptly named Cemetery Ridge.

Arthur could not use his field glasses any more; he could not bear to see men die in close up. He watched the senior officer with his hat lifted on his sword reach the stone wall just to the front of where Arthur was standing. The man paused and turned to shout to his men, when a bullet felled him. He had crossed a mile of hell, the air of which had been filled with lead and iron but he had not been touched. At this last moment his bravery was rewarded with death but he had brought his men to where they were most wanted - at the enemy's throat.

But it was not enough. There were too many fallen rebels behind these few who had reached the high point. They in their turn were swamped and there they died or were taken prisoner.

Behind them over the mile of sloping grass fields lay hundreds even thousands of men whose blood was seeping into that soil. Some were limping or crawling back to their lines, some were lying in agony with their wounds, screaming or in the silence of shock just before they died. They would shortly join the masses of bodies that had been torn from life and slammed into death.

The remnants of the Greys were retreating back to the woods. Arthur could clearly see a man in light grey seated on a grey horse, ride out towards these returning soldiers. With his binoculars Arthur was sure that it was General Robert E. Lee himself. He was surrounded by survivors who were attacking him? No, they were waving their arms in the air and they were cheering him!

Arthur put up his hand to steady himself against one of the trees in the small clump. It was in horror that he looked out at the enormous area of ground sweeping away down to the far woods.

Over half a mile wide and a mile in depth the battlefield was a mass of tortured humanity. The nearer part was coloured with blues and greys – and red. He could see it gently heaving like ripples on water as the men living, wounded or dying, moved individually. Their personal agony of movement, mixed in with the gun smoke, formed to create the macabre illusion of a lake.

Looking at that terrible field, he could also hear the full range of sound of man's emotions: the cheering and laughter below him of the Federal soldiers congratulating themselves on being alive and killing a lot of Rebs; the shouting of orders to prepare for a further attack; mixed with this the groaning of the wounded, pleading for assistance; the terrible cries of the mutilated wounded, who sought help but would accept death, anything to relieve the agony of their wounds; and above all the silence of the dead as they lay in droves across the

Rutland's Blues and Greys

fertile ground. All he could see was trampled green grass spaced with the grey brown of the soil and there contrasting was the red of blood draining wasted into the soil, when it should be pumping round the veins of these men.

Is Dan'l in there? Hancock had said it was Pickett's Brigade that was the main force.

As the sounds and sensations swept over him, he felt himself slipping into a terrible despair. What will man be prepared to do to his brother? Why does God allow this horror to happen?

Gradually he felt the tears come; they dropped from his eyes and rolled down his cheeks. He made no attempt to wipe them away but let them fall onto the soil as though in a vain attempt to wash away the blood that had been shed; to expiate the woe and suffering.

From behind him he heard his name being called. "Arthur." Slowly he turned his head to see Lawrence Chamberlain limping up to him.

Chamberlain saw the tear-stained face. "Arthur, are you hurt?"

Arthur dropped his head as the tears continued to fall. "What's the matter?" asked Lawrence.

Arthur raised his arm to point towards the plain of death. "Look!" he said, then with the tone of his voice dropping away, he repeated. "Look."

Chamberlain, the Professor of Debate and Rhetoric, understood - but he was without words to reply. He moved close to Arthur and gently placed his hand on Arthur's shoulder.

"Oh, my friend," he said. "My very dear friend." There was nothing he could say to this toughened professional soldier, who had suddenly seen that the worst that man can do to his brother was not to be borne. He turned away from the clump of trees on the top of Cemetery Ridge, and the British Artillery Colonel whose heart was breaking, and limped down the slope and back to his regiment.

Arthur took out his handkerchief and wiped his eyes. He stood upright and turned around from the battle scenes for he knew what he was going to do - he could not fight his inner feelings any more. He would go back to his tent and pack his saddlebags. Then he would ride back to Washington, write his reports and finally take a ship to England. It would be an end to his career but he was going home – he was going back to Millie.

He started to walk down the slope to his tent leaving the small group of trees, the very group at which General Lee had told General Longstreet to aim the centre of the Confederate Army.

Epilogue..

Arthur felt a hand shaking him.

"Wake up, Arthur." He opened his eyes and saw Millie leaning over him. He reached up and held her face in his hands. Then he kissed her on the lips. "Oh Millie, I do love you so."

Her lovely face broke into a gentle smile and her brown eyes looked at him with a returned love. "Well, that's a beautiful welcome."

Arthur looked around and then realised that he was still in his leather, high-back chair, and that he must have fallen asleep "But did they not hear anything?" he asked.

"Yes," she replied. "They know it all. I let them read your letters – all of them."

Peter said. "You'd told us about Fredericksburg - then you fell asleep. Mother showed us your letters after that, plus the letters from Jonathan and Abigail. I'm so very proud of you, Father."

Georgia knelt beside his chair and held his hand. "We felt your torment after those terrible battles."

He felt her tears on the back of his hand and reached across with his other hand to stroke her head. She lifted her face to him. "Oh Father Rutland, you're a wonderful man."

He smiled at Georgia and then turned his head to look up at his wife. Her kind and gentle face shone with its beautiful, welcoming smile.

'I did the right thing,' he thought. 'I ruined my career - but I came home to Millie.'

The American Civil War

For four years this terrible civil war ravaged the main part the country, and from the very start there was a steep learning curve for the whole nation. At the first battle at Bull Run in 1861, civilians from Washington had come out with their families and their picnics to watch the battle. When the Union Army was defeated, they swiftly found that there was death on the battlefield as they tried to flee on roads full of their own retreating army.

Both armies were initially based very strongly on patriotic volunteers. They flocked to the colours as well as forming their own military groups. It is amazing that batteries, companies and regiments were founded by amateurs who gathered like-minded men together. Sometimes the founder was given the colonelcy of the regiment he created, which in certain cases led to catastrophic disasters due to ignorance of basic military requirements.

Captain Reynolds created and led an efficient battery and went on to be a quality senior officer.

Lt Col Joshua Lawrence Chamberlain learned his military trade quickly and with incredible courage and determination became a senior and much respected General.

At the start both North and South drew its senior officers from the same main source, West Point Military Academy. The South appears initially to have had the best of the bunch - Lee, Longstreet, and Jackson - all of whom were top-quality generals.

The North had McClellan, who was a good organiser, able to weld an army together, equip and train it, but had little aggressive instinct. He was like a boy who has built a lovely toy but does not want to play with it in case it breaks. Hooker appears to have had some spirit (at times alcoholic spirit) but seems to have lacked strategic expertise. Meade was competent but not very imaginative, while Burnside was, in British Army terms, a GOPSM - a Grossly Over-Promoted Sergeant Major. He appears to have had little foresight, no ability to assess a military situation and failed to keep in touch with events on the battlefield, and was careless of his men's lives.

From these horrendous times new inventions flowed and often were tried out with success. The range is wide and often were the start of the future. Examples are:- the Gatling machine gun patented in 1862; signalling by flags -the 'wigwag' system; breech-loading rifles; transport of troops by rail; use of electric telegraphy; the submarine; steel-clad monitor ships; observation balloons for artillery spotting; formation of a medical corps and the Letterman ambulances - over 1000 ambulances were used at Gettysburg where they removed more than 14,000 wounded from the battlefield; and the Medal of Honor for all ranks.

Most of these new ideas and concepts originated in the North, but, though they developed the construction of many very efficient artillery pieces, they seemed to have completely forgotten the principle of using them as an arm.

End Thoughts, Acknowledgements & Historical information

This historical novel is based on the facts as I could find them and from the information I have found.

The reader will have seen that I show, through Arthur, I am highly critical of General Burnside's appalling actions at Antietam and Fredericksburg. I personally feel that he was a disaster that led to hundreds of unnecessary deaths, though there are a number of people who consider him a hero. Maybe my views should just be considered as a case for the prosecution.

I worry that this book is too gunnery centred and should in fact be called "The use and misuse of artillery at the battles of Antietam, Fredericksburg and Gettysburg." To me it is amazing that the lack of coordination of the Union artillery arm and the infantry should have been so great.

Roger Carpenter

What if? - What then?

At Antietam, what if Burnside had used two or three batteries against the defenders of the bridge for an hour before the attack and continued the barrage while the infantry were crossing the bridge? Almost certainly he would have been able to send his whole force across the Antietam well before midday and so attack the Confederate weak right wing - what then?

At Fredericksburg, what if artillery had been used against the stone wall? In my amateur view the result would have been the same because General Lee's defensive system was impenetrable, especially his left wing on Marye's Heights above the town. Burnside was out of touch with reality.

At Gettysburg, what if the Confederate barrage had been properly sighted and handled and only lasted an hour? It could have achieved much more damage by using fewer pieces that had been accurately ranged and so would have damaged the Union infantry lines lower down Cemetery Ridge. It would also have saved enough ammunition to cover the first half of Pickett's advance just prior to the actual charge, and also damage the Union lines again. I feel that Arthur was right in thinking that the Confederate army would have broken the Federal lines and reached the top of Cemetery Ridge, right in the centre of the Union position - what then?

Acknowledgements

I was given great assistance by a number of people when researching.

I am very grateful to the following organisations and people for answering all my questions so quickly and in such amazing detail:

US National Park Service at Antietam National Battlefield

and also at Fredericksburg and Spotsylvania NMP

The Central Library of Rochester and Monroe County

National Railway Historical Society, Philadelphia

Richard Henderson of L Battery Re-enactment

Anthony John - who proof read, advised and assisted with the editing – a long hard job.

And my thanks especially to the two very good American friends who suggested I read one of the most highly acclaimed Civil War books, 'Killer Angels' by Michael Shaara. I followed this with 'Gods and Generals' by his son Jeff Shaara. No one can fail to be inspired by these two books.

All factual mistakes or errors you might find in this story are of my accidental making.

Historical Information

Colonel Joshua Lawrence Chamberlain

This remarkable man survived Gettysburg and went on to win fame and glory. He was awarded the Congressional Medal of Honor for his action on Little Round Top. A little later on he was very badly wounded, being shot through both hips and not expected to live. He survived and, though wounded a further five times, was eventually promoted to Major General. He was elected Governor of Maine three times and also elected President of Bowdoin College. He died at the age of 83, in June 1914.

General Hancock

Wounded at Gettysburg, he later found that his friend General Lewis Armistead had been mortally wounded at the same battle, and died at the highest point of advance. It was Armistead that put his hat on his sword and waved it for his men. Hancock survived the Civil War.

General Henry Hunt

In the years to follow Gettysburg, he was much frustrated by the lack of support for his very moderate attempts to modernise the Federal Artillery. It remained under the control of individual infantry commanders who failed to understand its attributes.

Captain John Reynolds.

His family were grocers at 151 Main Street, Rochester NY. He was the chief organizer of and, for more than a year and a half, the captain of the battery in the First New York Light Artillery Regiment. He was subsequently assigned to the Army of the Cumberland as chief of artillery of the Twentieth Army Corps. His brother First Lieut. G. H. Reynolds was commissioned as Captain took command of the battery and was wounded at Gettysburg.

L Battery

L Battery - Rochester Union Greys - recruited principally at Rochester, Palmyra and Elmira, was mustered in the United States service at Elmira, November 17, 1861. It served in most of the major battles of the eastern campaigns until it was mustered out and honourably discharged when commanded by Capt. George Breck, June 17, 1865, at Elmira.

See the excellent re-enactment website. http://www.geocities.com/reynoldsbatteryl/main.html

Colonel Sir Percy Wyndham

This amazing character survived the war. After being wounded at Brandy Station, he was given a final assignment with the Union Army to command the District of Columbia Cavalry Depot. He was mustered out of the Army on July 5, 1864.

After which he went on to live an incredible life. In New York he established a military school and then went to Italy to serve on Garibaldi's staff in 1866. He returned to New York and, with a chemist as partner, established a petroleum refining business but an explosion destroyed his main distillery.

He sailed for India and established a comic newspaper, plus an Italian opera company. He also married a wealthy widow. He tried logging teak in Burma and lost the profits of his India exploits. He became commander-in-chief of the Burmese army but he was eventually reduced to penury.

His final most amazing project was the construction of an enormous balloon - 70 feet high and 100 feet round. But in January 1879 it exploded when over 300 feet high with him aboard. At 46 he died, so ending an almost unbelievable life.

Willards Hotel, was founded by the Willard brothers in 1853. Situated on the corner of 14th Street and Pennsylvania Avenue, it was then virtually the most prestigious hotel in Washington. Abraham Lincoln stayed there prior to his inauguration in 1861. It was known for its quality food served in its splendid dining room.

Ulysses Grant, when President of the United States, used to enjoy a cigar and brandy in the hotel lobby, where he was often approached by political wheelers and dealers. He created a new word for these men when he called them 'lobbyists'.

In 1901 the son of Joseph Willard built a magnificent hotel on the site. This elegant Edwardian building was twelve stories high. It is now one of Washington's finest hotels and well worth a visit.

Taps Bugle call

General Butterfield was dissatisfied with the call for Extinguish Lights, feeling that the call was too formal to signal the day's end. So with the help of the brigade bugler, Oliver Willcox Norton, he wrote 'Taps' to honour his men while in camp at Harrison's Landing, Virginia, following the Seven Days' Battles. These battles took place during the Peninsular Campaign of 1862. The call, sounded that night in July 1862, soon spread to other units of the Union Army

You can hear this emotive bugle call on - www.arlingtoncemetery.net/taps.htm

Roger Carpenter

Napoleon 12 pounder.

This was the main Field Artillery workhorse of the Union Army. It was a bronze casting with a smooth bore of about 4-5 inches. The tube was 66 inches long and weighed 1227 lbs. It fired a range of projectiles including 12 lb solid round shot, shell with time fuse, case and canister.

With a powder charge of 2.5 lbs, it could fire solid shot up to 1600 yards and was a very safe weapon with very few barrels bursting. Because of its smooth bore, it was not an accurate piece at any great distance but for short-range work, especially using canister against attacking infantry, it was without peer.

The picture above is of a Napoleon Cannon situated by the clump of trees on Cemetery Ridge at Gettysburg. This is the exact spot that Longstreet instructed General Pickett to aim his attack at, and from where Arthur watched the whole charge whilst sheltering behind the largest tree.

Rutland's Blues and Greys

3-inch Rifle

This is the other workhorse of the Union Army Field Artillery and used by L Battery. The barrel was made of strips of wrought iron wrapped around an iron core. With the core removed, the ensuing tube was plugged at one end, then rolled out to 7 feet and the bore reamed out to a 3-inch bore rifled barrel which weighed only 816 lbs. It could fire a 9-pound shell up to 3000 yards, with a powder charge of only one pound, with great accuracy. The main projectiles were the Hotchkiss 8-pound shell or the 9-pound case. Firing canister was useless because the rifling upset the shotgun effect. For short range work against charging infantry, the case shell with a very short time fuse was used.

Again the picture is of a 3-inch Rifle on the battlefield at Gettysburg.

About the Author

Roger Carpenter was born and bred in Surrey, England. He is 70 years of age, married, with a son and daughter; they are also married and have produced four granddaughters and a grandson, who are the joy of his life.

He and his wife have, for the past 40 years, lived in an old farm house in the North Downs. He had a horticultural company for many years that was one of the very first Garden Centres in Great Britain. He retired in 1987 and now manages 100 acres of woodland that they bought in Kent some years ago.

During his National Service, he served in the Royal Artillery from 1953 to 1955. It was during his time as a Gunner that he developed an interest in military history.

As an avid reader of C.S. Forester, Alexander Kent and Bernard Cornwell, and a devotee of the eminent historian Professor Richard Holmes, he immersed himself in his main interest of late 19th and early 20th century military engagements and weaponry before writing "Rutland's Curse," his debut novel.

This was followed by "Rutland's Guns" based on the same officer, Peter Rutland serving with the Gunners in the Boer War. Now "Rutland's Blues and Greys" is the story of Peter's father as an observer in the American Civil War.